Trails to Love

Book 3 of the Summer Trails Series

Janessa Suderman

This book is a work of literary fiction. Some circumstances and characters may be loosely based on the author's recollection of true-life experiences; however names have been changed to protect privacy.

Scripture references are taken from the New International Version of the Holy Bible.

Cover and interior art and design by Jonathan Suderman.

ISBN: 1542491258
ISBN-13: 978-1542491259

ACKNOWLEDGMENTS

Thank you to my editors and beta-readers, especially Jonathan Suderman, Ruth Zimmerman and Amber Sokowin, for your insights and enthusiasm in this project.

To keep in touch and learn about up-coming books, I warmly welcome you to visit www.janessa.ca.

CONTENTS

DEDICATION

To Kevin, my father and the story-teller of my child-hood. Thank you for empowering me and enabling me to buy Dawn.
And to Dawn herself; my once-in-a-lifetime horse, and to the many beautiful trails we have ridden together.

CHAPTER 1
OVER THE LINE

Jessa Davies leaned against the rails of the round pen, watching intently. Inside, the brown and white horse galloped around and around, driven by the girl with the whip. His nostrils flared. Foam frothed at the corners of his mouth as the whip cracked again just behind him, the loud thwack resounding through the dusty air.

Jessa adjusted her cowboy hat over her long brown hair, flinching as the whip cracked yet again. She knew its lash wasn't actually hitting Polka-dot; just scaring him. As she shifted her position she heard the envelope crinkle in her pocket, reminding her it was there. She had found it in her staff mail slot before walking down to the barn, and told herself she would open it later.

"Ease up on him, now, Tiff." Hank instructed, his voice seemingly amplified from where he was perched on the top rail. "He knows you're the boss. Now let him catch his breath."

Tiff lowered the whip and stood still in the centre of the round pen. Sweat glistened on her brow, and she flipped her black braids over her shoulders, waiting.

Polka-dot stood panting, his sides soaked. Jessa could hear him breathing hard. He turned his ears towards Tiff, watching her nervously.

"That's it." Hank said, "He's paying attention to you now. Give him a pat, then we'll try putting the saddle on him."

Jessa shifted her weight from one cowboy boot to the other, hearing the envelope crinkle again. It was hot, standing in the late-august sun in jeans and a button-down shirt. As much as she would have liked to cool off in the barn, or jump in the creek, Jessa stayed where she was. It was Sunday; and one of her last chances to sponge up as much horsemanship knowledge from Hank as she could. By this time next week, camp would be over for the year and she would be headed back to school.

"Giddyap!" Tiff roared, lunging Polka-dot into action again. The horse plunged around her through the sand, stopping only when she let-up. Hank hopped off the top rail and carried a saddle over, handing it to Tiff. He murmured something to her, then climbed back up on the rails.

Tiff walked straight up to Polka-dot and swung the saddle onto him. He skittered to the side, writhing, but Tiff jerked his halter hard and barked, "Quit it! You stand still." Eyeing her nervously, Polka-dot quivered on the spot. Tiff yanked the cinch tight and stepped away, cracking the whip again to make him run.

Jessa glanced sideways at Hank. He was watching intently and stroking his white beard. Jessa couldn't see his eyes in the shade of his cowboy hat. She wondered why he didn't make Tiff be gentler on the horse.

Not that Tiff wasn't a skilled horseman. Over the summer they had worked together at Spruce Ridge Camp, Jessa had come to respect that she and Tiff had very different approaches to riding, and that was okay. Tiff was fearless, demanding perfection from any horse she encountered. That seemed to work for her, even though

Jessa sometimes thought Tiff was harder on the horses than necessary.

It had been so different a few weeks before, when Jessa herself had had the chance to train a young horse. Hank had coached her, too, but hadn't suggested putting Fairlight in the round pen to 'break' her. He had simply said, "You're going to ride Fairlight today". Jessa had put her in a stall and taken her time, lovingly saddling and bridling her. Gentle Fairlight had turned her head to nibble at the saddle, but hadn't complained. She trusted Jessa, even though she had never been saddled before.

It had been so easy when Jessa first sat on her back. Hank had held the lead-rope, and Jessa simply climbed into the saddle, as though she had done it a thousand times. Fairlight had stepped sideways, surprised, and nuzzled Jessa's leg; but that was all. No bucking, no kicking, no running, no fighting. Certainly no whipping or yanking. Hank and Jessa had gone right out on a trail ride together, Fairlight learning the commands as they went along. Now, a month later, Jessa felt like she and Fairlight were of one mind. They were in tune with each other and Jessa didn't want to ride any other horse.

Perhaps the difference was that Fairlight and Jessa had a close bond even before that, or maybe it was Fairlight's sweet temperament. Whichever the case, Jessa was glad she hadn't had to whip the sweet filly, or yell at her, or work her into a sweat, like Tiff was doing to Polka-dot.

Her mind wandering back to the envelope in her pocket, Jessa pulled it out and read the cover again. Her first name was written in black pen, with no indication of whom it was from. She didn't recognize the writing. There was no stamp, so it had clearly been hand-delivered, indicating it was from another staff member. Jessa ripped open the envelope and pulled out a sheet of paper with writing scrawled half-way down the page. She scanned the bottom, noting it was unsigned.

"How's she doing?" Someone said beside her. Jessa jumped and stuffed the letter back into her pocket. She hadn't noticed her friend Nate approaching and now he stood next to her, looking through the rails at Tiff.

"Okay, I think." Jessa answered.

"Looks like she's almost ready to get on his back, hey?" Nate motioned. Jessa glanced at him. His dark hair had grown over the summer, and hung in sloppy waves over his forehead. He never wore a cowboy hat, preferring to wear neon-coloured baseball caps.

Tiff marched up to Polka-dot, gathered up the reigns, and swung onto his back before he had a chance to protest. He leapt into action at once, bucking and galloping around the pen. Tiff kept her seat, her solid arms bracing the reigns.

"Soften your reigns, Tiff." Hank called out. "We don't want him hard-mouthed from the start." Tiff's dark brows were drawn together, her lips a tight, inexorable line.

"I can't believe the summer's almost over." Nate said. "It went by so fast, and now we only have one week left."

"I know." Jessa sighed. "But we may still have some excitement to look forward to. My little brother Kenny comes this week."

"Nice." Nate said. "I wonder whose cabin he'll be in?"

"I already checked with Ms. Sheila." Jessa said, referring to the camp director. "He's in with Jay and Erik."

"Jay, the worship leader?" Nate asked.

"And Erik." Jessa repeated.

"I wish Emily wasn't missing our last week." Nate said. "She has some lame family vacation."

"Yeah." Jessa said, thinking that she wouldn't really notice Emily's absence. Emily had always been so quiet and shy. "At least most of us are still here." She glanced over her shoulder to the arena, where Wade was riding his horse Bea.

Wade was the handsome cowboy who had captured her interest at the beginning of summer. He was a true horseman; tall, broad-shouldered, and blue-eyed. In the beginning of the summer Jessa thought they might become a couple, but Wade had fallen hard for Virginia, Hank's stunning niece. After Virginia had left, Wade had turned his attention back to Jessa, and she wasn't entirely sure how she felt about that.

With a start, Jessa realized Nate had been talking to her. She hadn't heard a word he said.

"Sorry, can you repeat that?" Jessa cut into Nate's tirade apologetically. "I totally zoned out."

"Oh. Sure, I was just saying my parents are being all weird lately." Nate said, shrugging off his hoodie and slinging it over his shoulder.

"Weird, how?" Jessa asked. She had met Nate's parents several times, as they were also volunteering at the camp. They were certainly stricter than Jessa's parents; but seemed to have a good relationship with their kids.

"They're being all secretive. I've heard them arguing a few times, then they stop talking the second I come in the room. Yesterday my mom had all these papers out, and she got all panicky and hid them when I walked in."

"What do you think is going on?" Jessa asked.

"I have no idea." Nate said, furrowing his brow. "Hopefully it's nothing bad. Anyway. Speaking of families; how come you didn't go home this weekend, like usual? Your family's acreage is pretty close, isn't it?"

"It's complicated." Jessa hesitated, fiddling with the edge of her cowboy hat. "Partly it's because it's the last week of camp. I thought I'd soak in as much horse time as I can. Plus I knew Hank was helping Tiff train Polka-dot, and I wanted to watch." She didn't mention that she was also trying to figure out what her feelings were for Wade.

Nate nodded, then lowered his voice. "Is it also because of your older brother?"

"Clark?" Jessa looked quickly at Nate. "What do you

mean?"

"Well, it must be kind of weird for you." Nate said, cracking his knuckles. Jessa flinched; she hated that sound. It made her squeamish. "How's Clark doing, anyway?"

"You should probably be asking Tiff that question." Jessa grumbled, looking back into the round pen. Now Tiff was forcing Polka-dot in tight circles, his head turned back almost to her knee, as she kicked his belly. "She sees a lot more of him than I do."

"Hmm." Nate turned to watch Tiff, too. "So I gather that it still bothers you that they're dating?"

"Shh!" Jessa glared at him, then looked quickly back at Tiff, who seemed too involved in her work to have overheard. "Let's walk." She gestured her head towards the horse paddock. Nate followed. Most of the horses were relaxing in the afternoon sun. She spotted Fairlight and went to pat her. Stroking the buckskin's neck, she exhaled and looked at Nate.

"Look." Jessa said. "I don't want to be a big debbie-downer about this. But-"

"But you wish Tiff wasn't dating your brother." Nate finished for her. Jessa sighed.

"Exactly." She ran her fingers through Fairlight's dark mane, trying to undo some of the tangles. "And yes that may have been part of my reason for not going home this weekend. If I went, Tiff would go too. It's not exactly relaxing to watch them cavorting around on the couch and pretending to think it's cute. Does that make me a horrible person?"

"Of course not." Nate said, rubbing Fairlight's forehead. "I'm sure its awkward for you. Especially since it happened so fast."

"The bottom line is, I don't think they're a good match." Jessa said forcefully. "Their interests, their personalities-"

"Aren't they both out-going, extroverted types?" Nate interrupted.

"I suppose." Jessa shrugged. "They're both more aggressive, I guess. But he's all into rock-punk-boy band partying, and she's a bumpkin-horse girl." Nate snorted with laughter, clapping a hand over his mouth. Fairlight startled a little, then leaned back into Jessa's embrace.

"Bumpkin?" Nate sniggered. "What's that supposed to mean?"

"Alright I admit that was uncalled for." Jessa cracked a smile. "Ever since they started dating, Tiff acts different around me."

"Are you fighting again, like earlier this summer?"

"No, no." Jessa shook her head. "We're getting along fine. Tiff acts like we're best friends. And that's the problem."

"You lost me." Nate said.

"Well, here it is." Jessa said. "Tiff and I get along just fine. We got over our differences earlier in the summer and learned to co-exist. We were civil. We get along as co-workers. However, now that she's dating my brother, she's started acting like we're BFFs." She spouted. "Best friends forever". She clarified when Nate looked at her blankly.

"So, she thinks you're best friends, but you're not." Nate summarized.

"Correct. In the three weeks they've been dating, Tiff has somehow managed to come stay over at my house every single weekend. She's pretending to be besties, so she has an excuse to come over. I know it's really to see Clark."

"Maybe she really thinks you're best friends." Nate pointed out.

"No." Jessa shook her head, impatiently. "She's over every weekend, buttering up my mom, acting all chummy, then ditching me the second Clark gets home from work. I mean, she sleeps over in my bedroom. She uses my shampoo, then there's none left for me. She borrows my clothes and they get all stretched out. It's too much!"

"Does she ask first?" Nate inquired.

"Sort of." Jessa shrugged. "She asks in a way that makes it hard to say no. 'You don't mind if I come over for the weekend, do you Jessa? I get so lonely'. Or, she'll hold up a sweater and say, 'You don't mind if I borrow this, do you?' while she's already putting it on. So I sound like a horrible person if I tell her no. Well, maybe I don't want her sleeping over in my room every single weekend, and borrowing my stuff, and acting all buddy-buddy. It makes me feel..." Jessa paused, searching for the right word.

"Used?" Nate offered. "Taken advantage of? Manipulated?"

"Yes, yes, and yes." Jessa signalled three check-marks into the air. "The other problem is Clark. He's not as devoted as she is, and I know my brother. I know he'll drop her and move on to the next girl. And then it will be all awkward for me, and I'll be the one who's supposed to pick up the pieces, even though I was against this relationship from day one."

"Just be straight with her. And him. Tell them how you feel about all this." Nate suggested.

"If only it were that simple." Jessa massaged her tense eyebrows. "I don't want to hurt her feelings. She doesn't have a ton of friends."

"You can speak the truth, in a loving way. You know that saying, the truth shall set you free?" Nate said hopefully.

"I guess." Jessa buried her face in Fairlight's mane. "I wish I didn't have to deal with this at all. I wish it would just go away."

"Hey, come on." Nate said, trying to cheer her up. "It'll all work out somehow. Come on, let's go see how she's doing on that paint-coloured horse." He led her back through the paddock towards the round pen.

"Hey guys!" Tiff called from Polka-dot's back, waving them over exuberantly as they approached. "Check out my new ride!" She kicked Polka-dot into a run and loped him around the pen like a pro. "See? I just refuse to take no for an answer!"

"That's exactly what I'm afraid of." Jessa breathed, leaning forward to slump against the rails.

CHAPTER 2
HOPE DEFERRED

Jessa had some time before dinner, so she left Nate at the round pen and went to catch Fairlight, thinking it would be nice to go on a trail ride. Once Fairlight was saddled and ready in her stall, Jessa glanced around slyly. No one was close by. She leaned against Fairlight's side and pulled out the mysterious letter. Smoothing the crumpled paper, she read.

Jessa,

I just want to encourage you today. You are an amazing person. Smart, funny, kind, and beautiful. It's been wonderful to get to know you, and I hope you realize what a treasure you are. You are quite the catch and you deserve a true hero; never stop believing that. :)

I pray for you every day, and ask God to watch over you and bless you.

Secretly Yours.

PS: I admit I sometimes hope I will be the one who catches your eye; but only if it's God's will, and only in his timing.

Jessa read the whole letter twice, her eyes glued to the page. Then, hearing someone coming, she stuffed the letter back into her pocket and looked up, pasting on a smile.

Wade strolled up the aisle between the stalls, and tipped his hat to her.

"Well hey there, Jessa. If it isn't the prettiest filly at the barn." He said, winking.

"Hey, Wade." Jessa said, blushing. She wondered if Wade had written the letter. He had certainly turned the charm back on over the past few weeks.

"You goin' out on Fairlight?" He said, scratching the filly's forehead. "You're sure doing an amazing job with her."

"Thanks." Jessa said, not sure how to answer. "Yes I'm going out for a little trail ride before dinner."

"Do you want some company? Bea could use the exercise." Wade offered, smiling hopefully.

"Um, I don't know-" Jessa stalled, not sure how to answer. "I was thinking maybe I'd go on my own. Fairlight needs to learn to go where I tell her, without any of her horse buddies around. You know? I don't want her to be herd-bound." She said quickly.

"No problem." Wade said, scuffing his cowboy boot along the ground. "Maybe another time."

"Yeah. Sure." Jessa adjusted Fairlight's bridle, not looking at Wade.

"So, you know there's the final staff banquet this Saturday night." Wade said nervously. "It's a formal thing, apparently."

"Oh, right. I heard that." Jessa said.

"It's supposed to be a pretty big deal. With a country band and fancy dinner and dancing and everything." Wade continued. "Are you going?"

"I was planning on it." Jessa said, shrugging.

"Maybe we could go together?" Wade said, trying to catch her eye. Jessa wasn't sure why but she just wanted to get away. Having Wade pay attention to her would have been a dream come true a few weeks ago, but now she felt awkward about it.

"Maybe. Let's figure that stuff out later in the week." Jessa unclipped Fairlight and backed her out of the stall. "See ya!" She swung on and trotted away, leaving Wade still standing in the aisle.

As she trotted across the barnyard, Nate waved at her. He had joined Hank at the top of the round-pen rails to watch Tiff. She didn't look back at Wade. *Apparently someone is not used to hearing a girl say no.* Jessa thought. *Well, he can wait. I need to think this all out.*

Jessa kept Fairlight at a trot all the way through the grassy meadow that stretched out before the barn. When she entered the shade of the forest, she slowed her to a walk. The smell of the crisp spruce trees always calmed her. Fairlight walked boldly, trusting as Jessa nudged her along the trail.

"Good girl." Jessa cooed, leaning forward to stroke the horse's neck and ruffle up her black mane. "You are such an angel, you know that?" Fairlight nickered in response, then bent her head down to snatch up some grass.

"Ah-ah." Jessa pulled Fairlight's head back up. "That's bad manners, girl."

Jessa sighed, thinking back to her conversation with Wade. *The thing is, I'm not sure I want to be with Wade after all,* Jessa thought to herself. *On the outside he seems like the perfect guy; good-looking, strong Christian, he's kind, and he obviously likes me. But he was so quick to drop me when Virginia was in the picture. Now he wants me back, and I'm supposed to fling myself into his arms?*

Jessa frowned, remembering seeing Tiff do just that to her brother the other night. Clark had come to pick her up in his station wagon, and Tiff had launched herself at him as though he was a soldier returning from war. *I wish Clark would just break up with her,* Jessa thought, frowning. *If Clark tells Tiff it's over, then this whole problem goes away. The sooner the better. This stress is wrecking my last week of camp!*

Jessa walked Fairlight around the lonely high-ropes

course and climbing wall. She chided herself as she passed the archery range. She had never pictured herself as the type to interfere in someone else's relationship, but this was her brother. And Tiff had no business butting in to her family.

"Whoa." Jessa gently pulled back on the reigns, realizing she had arrived at the chapel. Just the sight of it made her feel humbled. *Why am I stressing about trying to fix their relationship? If it's meant to be, it will be. Maybe I'm just meddling because I'm avoiding dealing with my own muddled love life. I should just stay out of Clark and Tiff's business and let the chips fall where they may. If I'm right; they won't last long. And I should be surrendering my love-life to God and trusting He'll bring the right guy along at the right time.*

The chapel door creaked opened and Jay leaned out. He cocked his head and raised an eyebrow, grinning.

"Jessa Davies." Jay said, stepping all the way out. "I thought it was you. I saw you through the window."

"Hey, Jay." Jessa smiled. Jay always seemed to be able to put her at ease. Maybe it was because he was older; nineteen and already finished his first year of college. He was a good buddy and she enjoyed joking around with him. Today his yellow dreadlocks flocked freely down his shoulders, and he wore a ratty t-shirt with the words 'Shalom Falls Bible College' peeling off the front. He wore multiple, threaded friendship bracelets; no doubt gifts from admiring campers throughout the summer.

"Is this the famous Fairlight?" Jay asked, looking at the buckskin.

"Yes." Jessa said proudly. "This is my sweetie."

"May I?" Jay stepped forward, stretching out a hand to pet her.

"Of course." Jessa said. "Say hi to Jay, girl." Fairlight smelled Jay's hand and allowed him to pat her neck.

"She's cute." Jay said.

"Thanks." Jessa said. "She's a sweetheart, too. I've only been riding her a few weeks, and she's never even bucked or anything." Fairlight stepped to one side. The crumpled envelope fell out of Jessa's pocket, fluttering to the ground near Jay's foot.

"What's that?" Jay crouched down to pick it up.

"No don't look at it!" Jessa yelped in a panic. "It's nothing. I-" Jay passed it to her without looking at it, and Jessa stuffed it back in her pocket. "Just an encouragement letter. From a friend. I didn't mean to jump down your throat."

"It's cool." Jay said, stepping back to look up at her. "Are you excited about singing on the worship team this week?"

"Yeah." Jessa said. "I'm glad it finally worked out." Jay had been bugging her to join the band all summer, but her barn schedule hadn't permitted it. She loved singing, and even took classical voice lessons during the school year. Finally Jay had personally asked Hank if he could let her off some of her barn duties so she could do both.

"The practices are right after breakfast, at nine." Jay reminded her. "So you'll still get to spend your afternoons at the barn."

"Perfect." Jessa nodded. "Oh, and hey, apparently you will have my little brother in your cabin this week. Kenny."

"Yeah, I saw that." Jay said, grinning. "Should be a fun time. Erik and I are tag-teaming. Gotta love those ten-year-olds." Fairlight was starting to fidget, standing still for so long.

"I better get back to the barn." Jessa said. "Fairlight wants her dinner."

"See you later." Jay stepped back. "Oh, by the way, I saw your friend Marsha at the lodge. She said to tell you she's back early and she'll see you at dinner."

"Okay." Jessa said. "Weird. I thought she was going to a wedding tonight. She wasn't supposed to be back till tomorrow morning."

"Well, enjoy the rest of your ride!" Jay waved as she

turned Fairlight barn-ward and urged her into an easy trot.

CHAPTER 3
OMISSION

The wranglers squeezed in at the support-staff table for dinner. Jessa pulled up a chair beside Jay, who was looking uncomfortable next to his college roommate, Russ, and Russ's girlfriend Cory-Lynn. The couple were tickling each other and feeding each other bites of French-fries.

Jessa plonked her plate down next to Jay, who looked enormously relieved. Jessa thought she heard him breathe, "Thank God", under his breath. Since Cory-Lynn had come into the picture earlier that summer, Jay was often left the third-wheel. Plus, the love-struck couple were not always discreet about their affection. More than once Jessa had joined the trio just so Jay would have someone to talk to.

"Hey." Jay said, scooting over to make more room. "Did you ever find Marsha?"

"She's in the food-line right now." Jessa gestured to where Tony, the cook, was dishing out dinner. "I haven't heard her news yet, though." Wade pulled up a chair opposite Jessa and gave her a tight smile.

"Where's everybody else?" Jay asked. "From the barn, I mean."

"Let's see." Jessa counted on her fingers. "Tiff took off on a date with my brother, Hank went home for the night, and Emily is on a family vacation."

"We've got a skeleton crew at the barn this week." Nate said, dipping his chicken-strips in ketchup and chomping into it. "Hey, Jessa, check it out." Nate motioned to his dad and mom, who were conferring at the next table. Their heads were bent over a binder, their expressions serious. "I'm telling you, they're up to something."

"Maybe they're just...planning your birthday party." Jessa guessed wildly. "Aren't you turning sixteen in a couple weeks?"

"Yes, but I doubt that's it." Nate said, staring at his dad suspiciously. "I think it's something else. Something bad."

"Why don't you just ask them?" Jay offered, taking a swig of juice. Nate shook his head, and stuffed more chicken-strips into his mouth.

"Can you guys believe this is the last week of camp? The final staff banquet should be a blast, hey?" Nate said, his cheeks bulging with food. "Are we supposed to pair off for that?" Jessa ignored him and bit into her fries. She didn't want to discuss pairing-off while Wade was present.

"Totally!" Cory-Lynn giggled. Cory-Lynn always giggled. "I think I can guess whom my escort will be." She winked at Russ.

"What are you guys going to do after the summer's over? Are you going to keep dating, long distance?" Nate said to her and Russ. "I mean, isn't your bible college like, three hours away from here?"

"Actually," Russ said, breaking into a sly smile, "Cory-Lynn's moving to be close to me."

"Really?" Jessa asked. She knew that Cory-Lynn was in her early twenties, like Russ, and still lived at home with her parents in Sun Valley. "You're moving out to Shalom Falls?"

"Isn't it wonderful?" Cory-Lynn giggled. "So romantic."

"I guess." Jessa took another bite of French-fry. She thought it seemed hasty, as the couple had only been dating six weeks.

"She's moving in with my Auntie Freya." Russ continued. "And getting a job at her daycare."

"Wow." Jessa said blankly. "How nice." She glanced at Jay, who was tucking into his chicken and fries. "Are you guys still going to be roommates this year?"

"Yep." Russ nodded. "Second year going strong." He high-fived Jay. Just then Marsha walked over, her plate piled high with salad. Marsha was Jessa's closest friend at camp, and was hard to miss: she was incredibly tall and thin, black, and had a bleach-blond pixie-cut.

"You're back early." Jessa said, scooting over to make more room. "Weren't you supposed to be at a wedding this evening?"

"Yes. I was." Marsha plonked her plate down dramatically. "And you'll never guess what happened."

"One of them got cold feet?" Nate guessed.

"Yes!" Marsha said, her jaw dropping as she slapped Nate on the shoulder. "How did you know that?"

"Just a guess." Nate said. "Was it the bride or groom?"

"The bride." Marsha said. "My cousin. I guess she's had second thoughts for a while, but then this morning she kept delaying putting the wedding dress on. Finally she realized she didn't want to put it on at all, and that was her clue. She didn't want to marry him, after all."

"Poor bloke." Russ said, wrapping his bony arm around Cory-Lynn's shoulders. "He must be heartbroken."

"This will make a lot of drama in the family, I tell you." Marsha said. "Apparently they were the 'golden couple'. No one saw this coming."

"Wow." Jessa said. "I can't imagine running out on my wedding day."

"Well, she says she's had some doubts and concerns all along. Kind of a nudging that something wasn't right, you know?" Marsha said, pouring dressing on her salad. "But she ignored it because he seemed like such a perfect match for her. Then today she said she couldn't go through with it."

"Is that what you wanted to talk to me about?" Jessa asked, so only Marsha could hear. "Jay said you were looking for me."

"Yep. I wanted to hash it all out. I guess we just did, though. So, I don't think there's anything else we need to talk about." Marsha said, taking a bite of salad.

"Yes, we do." Jessa said, lowering her voice even more. "After dinner. I need your advice."

"Ooooh." Marsha said giddily, dropping her fork and clapping. "Why do I get the feeling this will be juicy?"

"Shh!" Jessa glanced around the table, but no one seemed to be paying attention. She leaned closer to her friend, "Because it is!"

After dinner, Jessa and Marsha huddled upstairs in the staff lounge. They had it to themselves, and sat close on the faded floral couch, reading and re-reading the letter. Finally Marsha sat back.

"Hmm." Marsha said, a glimmer in her brown eyes. "How very interesting. Most interesting development indeed."

"I know!" Jessa stood up, the letter in one hand, and started to pace. "If it weren't for the post-script, I would almost have thought it could be from a girl. Just being nice, you know? But then, where he says he hopes it will be him..."

"This is so romantic." Marsha said. "I knew Wade

would take my adv- I, I mean-" Marsha clapped her hand over her mouth.

"Marsha!" Jessa pounced at her. "What did you say to Wade? Tell me!"

"Fine." Marsha said, smirking. "After Virginia left, Wade asked me if you would possibly still be interested in him. I said I thought maybe if he tried again, you would give him a chance."

"What!" Jessa flopped back on the couch. "When was this?"

"A week ago." Marsha said. "Yeah, it was really sweet. He said something about how he was all distracted by Virginia, but now that she's gone he realizes more than ever that you're the one he liked the whole time. He thought you'd never give him a second chance, but I said go for it. Nothing ventured, nothing gained."

"I can't believe this." Jessa said. "No wonder he's been so forward lately. He asked me to the banquet, you know."

"He obviously wrote this letter, too!" Marsha said, pointing. "It has to be! He's trying to woo you back."

"Maybe." Jessa said, running her hands through her hair. "I mean, probably, yeah, it was him."

"Well, who else could it be?" Marsha demanded.

"I don't know." Jessa admitted. "I'm not even positive I want to be with Wade, anymore. Is that crazy? Earlier this summer getting together with him was all I could think about, but now, something doesn't feel quite right."

"Jessa, you've never had a boyfriend before." Marsha said superiorly. "I have. I know when two people are good together. You and Wade are meant to be. You have so much in common. He adores you. This is so romantic."

"I guess." Jessa shrugged.

"Besides, no ones asking you to marry him. It's just a banquet. How will you know what it would be like to date him, until you try it?"

"I don't know." Jessa said, getting a headache. "I'm not ready to answer him."

"Good." Marsha nodded energetically. "Play hard to get. Let him dangle."

"You aren't helping." Jessa playfully tried to push Marsha off the couch.

Much later that night, Jessa woke up when the bedroom door opened, then closed. She rolled over in her sleeping bag, propping herself up on one shoulder to squint at the blinking digital clock. It was three am. On the other side of the room, she could hear Marsha's even breathing. The two girls had talked and played cards late into the evening, before finally going to bed at eleven.

"Tiff?" Jessa whispered in the darkness.

"Yeah?" A voice answered near the door. Jessa heard Tiff kicking her shoes off and shrugging out of a coat.

"Are you just getting back from your date with Clark?" Jessa whispered.

"It was so fun." Tiff said. Jessa could hear her wriggling out of her jeans. "Your brother is just the hottest."

"Tiff," Jessa groaned. "It's three o clock in the morning."

"I know." Tiff said. "I was trying to open the door quietly. Sorry I woke you."

"Curfew is at eleven pm." Jessa said simply. Tiff didn't answer. Jessa could hear her rummaging in her bag, probably trying to find her pyjamas.

"Tiff, you know we aren't supposed to be out past eleven. You promised Hank earlier this summer you'd respect that."

Tiff huffed out an impatient sigh. "Come on, Jessa." She whispered. "Don't be such a goody-goody. It's the last week of camp."

"What were you doing?" Jessa quizzed.

"I was with your brother, you worry-wart." Tiff

whispered, forcing a chuckle. "I was perfectly safe."

"You could get in trouble." Jessa said quietly. "If Hank or Ms. Sheila finds out-"

"They won't." Tiff said swiftly. "No one knows but you, and you wouldn't tattle on me, would you?" Jessa didn't answer. She stared straight above her, knowing that the slats of the bunk above were a few feet overhead, though she couldn't see them. Over the years staff had carved their names into it, and it had been painted over several times, though it still showed the grooved initials. But now all she could see was blackness.

"Jessa?" Tiff hissed, sounding more worried. "You won't rat me out, will you? Promise me. We're friends. You're like, my best friend."

Jessa sighed irritably. "Good-night, Tiff." She rolled back over to the wall and curled up in a ball. Tiff said something else, but Jessa stuffed her pillow over her head so she couldn't hear it.

CHAPTER 4
NEW ADDITIONS

The next morning, Cory-Lynn slopped steaming oatmeal into Jessa's bowl, and she doctored it liberally with cream and brown sugar before heading to the wrangler table. Everyone else was already there, except for Marsha. She had still been in the shower when Jessa came down to breakfast.

"Morning, Jessa." Hank said as she sat down. "Good. Now that you're here, I have a few announcements."

"Marsha's not here yet." Jessa said, looking towards the dining room door. She saw Russ tickling Cory-Lynn over the counter; but no Marsha.

"That's okay." Hank said, taking a sip of coffee. "We'll get started without her. As you all know we will be a bit short staffed this week, so I've called in some extra barn help to cover the workload."

"How did we get so short?" Tiff asked after chugging her glass of milk.

"Well, of course Emily had to leave, and Jessa has morning worship practice." Hank took another sip of his coffee.

"Who'd you get?" Tiff asked. "Is Virginia coming back?" Jessa blanched, hoping the answer was no. She stole a glance at Wade, who was sipping his coffee intently, his expression unreadable.

"No, unfortunately my niece is busy on the rodeo circuit all week." Hank said. "She's going for Rodeo Princess again. So she can't come back. But my wife Barb is helping out, and we're also getting Patrick. He's on the maintenance team. He's not exactly experienced, but beggars can't be choosers, and he was willing." Hank pointed over to the next table, where Patrick was gobbling orange slices as though it was his last meal. Patrick wasn't exactly Jessa's favourite person. She had only talked to him once or twice all summer, and had found him to be extremely annoying. Maybe it was because he always seemed to assume she had a mad crush on him, which she did not.

"Your wife is coming?" Nate looked confused. "I thought she had to stay home and take care of your ranch this summer?"

"It's just for a few days." Hank said, chuckling. "Barb is my angel. She's a wonder with horses."

"Has she ever worked at camp before?" Nate asked.

"No, she prefers a quieter life." Hank said mildly. "She's a real artistic soul; a poet, really. She doesn't spend much time around other people. Except for me, of course. But she's coming and I know you're all going to love her." Hank said.

After breakfast Hank went to pick up his 'angel.' Instead of walking to the barn with the others, Jessa hung around the lodge and walked over to the chapel with Jay and Russ. It felt strange to miss the morning at the barn, but it was also a nice change.

Worship practice ended up being a lot of fun. Jay made it obvious he was ecstatic she had finally joined, after being ribbed about it all summer. He gave her a solo part in one of the main worship songs, saying, 'Those campers are gonna want your autograph'.

Cory-Lynn had come to watch the practice after clearing up the breakfast dishes; flushed and perched in the front row, watching Russ adoringly. Cory-Lynn looked so star-struck that once or twice Jessa glanced at Russ, half-expecting to see he had transformed into a handsome, muscular knight in shining armour. However, he was as gangly and awkward as ever, with his buzzed head and prominent Adam's apple. He certainly seemed happy, though.

After practice, Jessa walked out to the barn. She was keen to meet Hank's wife. Marsha said Barb was in the horse paddock, so Jessa wandered that way to introduce herself. She breathed in the familiar musty scent of hay and manure. Zorro and Peaches were blocking her view of most of the herd. Jessa brushed past them and stepped around Rocky, then stopped short.

A short stranger stood amongst the herd; her arms outstretched and her face heaven-ward. The stranger wore a faded leather slicker, despite the sunny weather, and a battered cowboy hat. Her face was tanned and lined, like Hank's.

"Hi!" Jessa stepped forward with a friendly smile. Barb slowly lowered her gaze until it rested on Jessa. Her expression didn't change and Jessa was struck by an intense look in her glittering eyes.

"I'm Jessa." Jessa continued. "You must be Hank's wife Barb, I take it?"

Again Barb didn't answer, but continued to look at Jessa intently, arms still raised. Jessa had the strangest feeling that Barb could read her thoughts.

Then, in a low, gravelly voice, no louder than a whisper, Barb began to speak, her eyes fixed on Jessa.

To hellos and goodbyes and in betweens
To unveil the truth where it is unseen
To trust and let go of a weakly fire
To await the blaze of the heart's desire.

An eerie wind blew through the paddock then. Jessa's heart was thumping loudly in her chest and her neck tingled; though she wasn't sure why. Barb said nothing more, but Zorro and Peaches pricked up their ears at the wind, and trotted over to Barb. Leviathan and Rocky followed, and then Polka-dot and Buster. The six horses formed a circle around Barb, blocking her partially from view, and then, almost as one, the horses began to walk in a clock-wise circle. Through the ring of horses, Jessa saw Barb raise her hands slightly higher, and all six horses broke into a smooth trot, encircling Barb.

Jessa couldn't help it; her jaw dropped. She had never seen horses behave that way. It was as though Barb could control them with just her thoughts.

"You met my angel, I see?" Jessa jumped, startled out of her trance. Hank was trudging up next to her, leading his horse Silver. "That's my Barb."

"How does she do that?" Jessa murmured. Hank chuckled.

"Barb's always had a special gift with horses. Understands them, you know? Speaks their language."

"Wow." Jessa said. "Amazing."

"Yes she is." Hank said fondly, watching his wife. Four other horses had joined the circle and all ten were trotting smoothly around Barb, like a living whirlpool. "Come on, let's get to the barn. We've got work to do."

Jessa followed Hank to the gate, but stopped when she felt a horse nuzzling her arm. She turned and saw it was Fairlight.

"Hi, sweetheart!" Jessa beamed, giving the buckskin a hug around the neck. "You didn't want to join the merry-go-round?" Jessa saw that more than half the herd was trotting around Barb. Fairlight, however, ignored them entirely and whinnied softly at Jessa.

"Would you look at that." Hank said admiringly. "Apparently this little filly knows where her allegiance lies." Jessa glowed and gave Fairlight a final pat before following Hank into the barn.

After completing the morning chores, the wranglers walked up to lunch together. Wade walked beside Jessa and struck up a conversation with her. Jessa played along, laughing and joking as best she could, and wondering what had happened to the magic that had once been between them. More importantly, she wondered if she would ever get it back.

CHAPTER 5
KENNY

Jessa didn't return to the barn with the others after lunch. She had asked Hank if she could stay back and say hi to her family first. Just after one o clock they arrived, her dad Eugene carrying Kenny's back-pack and sleeping bag. Nancy was assuring him he would have a great time, and Kenny himself fairly wriggled with excitement.

"Jessa!" Kenny launched himself at her. Smiling widely, Jessa opened her arms to hug her little brother. Instead of hugging her, Kenny ducked under her arms and tried to tickle her ribs.

"Ow, ooh, hey!" Jessa writhed out of his reach. "Kenny!"

"Gotcha!" Kenny giggled.

"Good grief." Jessa rolled her eyes as Kenny sped on ahead to Cabin Three. Jessa followed with her parents, rubbing her ribs.

"To say he's excited is an understatement." Nancy said, squeezing Jessa into a side-hug as they walked. "He wants you to take him on a trail ride."

"Sure." Jessa said ominously. "As long as he's not

planning some mischief."

"Can't promise that." Eugene winked at her and squeezed her shoulder. "We're looking forward to having our girl home with us after this week. It's been a lonely summer!"

"Aw dad." Jessa kicked the ground. "I can't believe its almost over." They reached Cabin Three to find that Kenny had already introduced himself to Jay, and was swinging from the porch rafters.

"Hey." Jay smiled and reached to shake hands with Eugene and Nancy. "You must be Kenny's parents, I take it? I'm Jay. And we have another counsellor, Erik, but he's just over at the office right now."

"Nice to meet you, young man." Nancy said. "I've heard a lot about you from Jessa." Jay looked pleased, which embarrassed Jessa for some reason. She didn't want her parents to get the wrong idea.

"I told them you're the worship leader." Jessa interjected. "And how I'm in the band this week."

"Right-on." Jay beamed as Kenny darted inside the cabin. "Your daughter is very talented, ma'am."

"That's very true." Nancy said, approvingly, then gave Jessa a sly look. "So tell me, Jay, what do you get up to when you're not at camp?" Jessa slipped inside where Kenny had claimed a bunk-bed.

"Hey, kiddo, how's it going? You excited to go riding with me?" Jessa grabbed Kenny's shoulders and jostled him.

"Hey!" Kenny sprang for her knees, trying to squeeze them. Jessa jumped aside and tripped over Kenny's back-pack, which had been dropped on the cabin floor. She fumbled, trying to regain her balance just as Jay and her parents entered. Her arms flailing wildly, she toppled and collided straight into Jay's chest.

"Ooof!" Jay said, catching her. "Easy does it! You okay?"

"Yeah." Jessa said, disentangling her feet from

Kenny's bag. Her cheeks were flaming red. She didn't look up at Jay but was acutely aware of how strong his chest had felt as she smashed her face against it; and the fresh scent of his aftershave. "Well, I better get going to the barn. See you guys later!" Jessa edged towards the door.

"Bye honey! We'll pick you up Saturday evening after the banquet." Eugene waved at her. She waved back and started jogging towards the barn.

Jessa felt a little light-headed as she entered the barn-yard. The trail horses were already saddled and waiting in their stalls for the afternoon trail rides. Someone had saddled Fairlight, too. Jessa paused in front of her stall, puzzled. Normally no one handled Fairlight except for herself, and she wanted to keep it that way.

Frowning, Jessa scratched Fairlight's forehead and breezed into the barn, looking for Hank. She found Nate in the tack-room.

"Hey, Nate." Jessa said loudly. "Do you know why Fairlight is saddled?" Nate looked at her blankly and shook his head.

"No idea." He said and walked out with a saddle. Huffing, Jessa stalked to the office. Tiff and Patrick were there, going over the assignment board. Patrick turned to look at her, his eyes beady in his flabby face. Jessa felt a familiar wave of irritation that she always felt when he was around.

"Well look what the cat dragged in." Patrick wheezed. "I thought you didn't even work down here anymore, you slacker."

"I do." Jessa said curtly, stepping around Patrick to look at the board. He smelled like feet. "Tiff, why is Fairlight saddled?" Jessa demanded.

"Cause I'm 'unna ride her." Patrick said, puffing out his chest before Tiff could respond.

"No, you're not." Jessa snarled. "No one rides Fairlight but me."

"She's not yours." Patrick taunted, clearly enjoying

this. "Last I checked she's a camp horse."

"How dare-" Jessa flared up, but Tiff cut her off.

"He's just kidding, Jessa. It was just a joke." Tiff said firmly. "Barb saddled her for you. Hank asked her to. Patrick is riding Rocky."

"Oh." Jessa backed down. "Sorry." Patrick shook his head at her, chuckling.

"You really gotta lighten up, Jessa. Does somebody have major PMS hormones today?" He said.

"I'm warning you, Patrick." Jessa growled.

"Hey, calm down. That rage ain't doin' nobody any good." Patrick laughed, standing closer to her face than she would have preferred. "Incidentally, I like a gal who's got some fire. Say, what do you say we kick things up a notch?"

"What?" Jessa asked, disgusted.

"You heard me." Patrick repeated, his breath dank. "Let's try us out. I've had my eye on you, and you've got a spicy temper. Me likey. Go with me to the banquet?" Tiff sniggered.

"Forget it, Patrick!" Jessa spat.

"Come on. I could be your hero." He said, unflinching. The blood drained out of Jessa's face.

"What did you say?" She whispered, remembering the anonymous letter she had found in her mail slot. Hadn't the writer said something about her deserving a hero?

"That's right." Patrick said, clearly pleased. "You're the damsel in distress, and I'm your hero. I don't give up easy. That's why we belong together." Tiff was red in the face, chortling into her hand. Non-plussed, Patrick stepped even closer and held out a pudgy hand toward her.

"No!" Jessa turned and stomped out of the office, thinking, *Man, that guy gets under my skin! I can't believe that jerk wrote me that letter! And here I thought it was from Wade. What a joke!*

Jessa went on two trail rides that afternoon. Barb led the first ride and Jessa rode flank. Again, Barb did not speak, but maintained a relaxed silence. The campers didn't seem to mind. Barb exuded a calm confidence, and somehow it was comforting. Jessa didn't feel like talking either, so she sat back on Fairlight and took in the sights and smells of the forest; the chirping of birds and gentle swaying of green branches. The forest had a slightly sweeter smell than it had at the beginning of summer; Jessa knew it was the grasses and leaves starting to decay. The forest was no longer fresh, but was starting to die as autumn approached.

As she rode, she thought back to the incident with Patrick. Perhaps she had been a little insensitive; rebuffing his attention so harshly. But the thought of him riding Fairlight had instantly put her in a furious mood. The harsh reality was setting in that Fairlight belonged to the camp, and after Jessa left, Fairlight would be at the mercy of whichever wrangler or camper wanted to ride her. *She'll be ruined.* Jessa thought, dread filling her. *I've trained her to be so gentle and good, and someone will yank her and kick her and whip her; and campers will confuse her, and she'll be a ruined, numb, hard-mouthed horse. How can I leave her?*

For the second trail ride, Kenny was in attendance. He had already made friends with two other boys in his cabin, and the three were a vortex of energy. Jessa led that ride, and put Kenny on Zorro, the tallest black horse in the herd. She felt proud that he didn't seem nervous at all, and sat bolt upright on Zorro's back. She wondered if he and his friends might cause trouble, but aside from their non-stop chatter the ride was uneventful. At the end of the ride she had Kenny stay on Zorro for a few extra minutes while she grabbed the camera from the office and snapped a few pictures of him.

Kenny was so happy; so free of the pressures and stress weighing on Jessa. She felt a little jealous. His unencumbered, joyful face lighting up for the camera as he gave a thumbs up and beamed. Her lucky brother had no idea how easy he had it; just pure, kid-style fun at camp. As

Jessa took a few more pictures, she signed wistfully, thinking, *If only my life were so simple.*

CHAPTER 6
CHAPEL

Worn-out and cranky, Jessa got to chapel a few minutes early that evening to help Jay set up the microphones. He had tied a bandana around his head to keep the dread-locks out of his face.

"You all set for this?" He asked her.

"Yeah." Jessa grumbled, adjusting her music stand.

"Everything okay?" Jay asked, looking at her.

"Yeah. Fine." Jessa said. "Let's do this."

"It's normal to feel a bit nervous the first time you-"

"I'm not nervous." Jessa flashed, then instantly regretted her tone, seeing the startled look on Jay's face. "Sorry. I mean, I just have some stuff on my mind."

"Do you want to talk about it? We have a few minutes." Jay offered.

"Not really." Jessa said. "It's too complicated." Jay looked at her evenly for a moment, evaluating her response.

"It's your call." He said kindly. "If you ever want to talk about it, I'm here, alright?"

"Thanks." Jessa said automatically, flipping through

the sheets of worship music. Russ and the rest of the band joined them a minute later, and Jay gathered them all in a circle to pray before chapel. Jessa tried to focus on his prayer instead of her swirling thoughts.

"Lord, we're here." Jay said simply. "We're here because you've called us to be at this camp, on this worship team, and we know you have a reason and a plan for that. We love you. We want to honour you and thank you; for who you are, and what you've done in our lives. We're so thankful, Lord. And I ask you to bless every person on this team. Whatever we're going through in our lives, help us set it aside so we can come and worship you, Father. We know you are in control, and that you love us more than we can imagine. Please help us to trust you. Help us get rid of the distractions so we can bring you our best selves. Thank you Jesus. Amen."

Jessa got in position as Jay went to open the doors. The campers streamed in, rushing to get the best seats. Kenny and his friends came in with Erik and made a bee-line for the front row; right under Jessa's nose.

"Hey, Jess! There's my sister!" She heard Kenny proclaiming to anyone who would listen.

"All righty campers!" Jay yelled into the microphone, "Who's ready to worship God tonight?" The drummer hammered out a solo as the campers went wild. From there they went straight into a fast-paced worship song. Jessa sang and couldn't help laughing at Kenny and his friends jumping around in the front row. He looked like he was having a blast.

Jesus, we love you (we love you)
You are our saviour (our saviour)
We will follow you (follow you)
Til the end of time
Jesus, you are our King (our King)
The mighty warrior (mighty warrior)
Our praise to you we bring (we bring)
With all our hearts

You make us so happy, and we'll sing it all day long
You fill up my cup, It overflows with joy!

After three or four more fast-paced songs, it was time for Jessa's solo. Jay strummed quietly on his guitar, bringing the energy level down. Jessa took a steadying breath and sang into the microphone.

Lord, you are in control
You never let me go
I will trust in you, trust in you
You know what's best for me,
You give me perfect peace
I will trust in you, trust in you.
When my world falls apart
I know you hold my heart
Giving me a brand new start
I will trust in you, trust in you.

As she sang Jessa felt somewhat hypocritical. Over the past few days she had been so anxious about keeping control; and she had forgotten to trust God to look after her. When she sang through it a second time, with the campers joining in, she sang from the heart.

When it was time to sit down, she looked over to the barn-staff pew; but it looked like the only available spot was next to Patrick. Tiff was missing. Jessa opted to sit with Jay and Kenny up front rather than join the wranglers.

Russ stayed on stage and selected an audience member to come read a bible verse. A young girl in overalls bounded up to the front, her blond pony-tail swishing as Russ showed her what to read, and adjusted the microphone for her.

"Okay. I got it." The girl said, holding open the bible.

"First, what is your name?" Russ asked.

"Kelly McKnight!" She said breathily, her hands trembling with the open bible. "Should I read it now?"

"Go for it!" Russ encouraged and stepped back. Jay held his open bible closer to Jessa so she could follow along.

"Okay." Kelly said, clearing her throat. "Ecclesiastes 3:1-12: There is a time for everything, and a season for every activity under the heavens:

a time to be born and a time to die,
a time to plant and a time to uproot,
a time to kill and a time to heal,
a time to tear down and a time to build,
a time to weep and a time to laugh,
a time to mourn and a time to dance,
a time to scatter stones and a time to gather them,
a time to embrace and a time to refrain from embracing
a time to search and a time to give up,
a time to keep and a time to throw away,
a time to tear and a time to mend,
a time to be silent and a time to speak,
a time to love and a time to hate,
a time for war and a time for peace."

"Let's hear it for Kelly!" Russ bellowed. Kelly curtsied and skipped back to her seat, as Bill, the chapel speaker stepped up to the front. He spoke for the next twenty minutes, sharing the gospel and explaining how God had sent his son Jesus to die for them, and pay for their sins, so they could be with God forever in heaven. Jessa pondered the verses Kelly had read.

A time for everything, Jessa pondered. *A time to leave camp, and leave Fairlight; and leave this whole summer behind her. A time to go back to school and move on with life. A time for goodbyes.*

When chapel was over, Jessa was helping Jay tidy the stage when she heard a loud 'Pssst! Jessa over here!' Jessa looked over the crowd of departing campers. They were all heading to snack, no doubt, and then they would have cabin devotional time before bed.

"Jessa! Down here!" The voice whispered again. Jessa spotted Nate, crouching on his hands and knees behind the front row bench.

"What?" Jessa said boredly, unplugging her microphone.

"Come here." Nate gestured.

"Why?" Jessa said.

"I need your help! Just, come on!" Nate whispered. Rolling her eyes, Jessa strolled over to where Nate crouched and sat down near his hiding place.

"Okay, let me guess. You want to play a prank on someone and I'm supposed to help?" Jessa whispered.

"No, not this time." Nate whispered. "I need your help with something."

"You said that." Jessa countered, her curiosity growing. "What?"

"You know how my parents are being all weird lately?" Nate said, his voice a low murmur. He stole a glance over at his dad, Fred, who stood near the sound booth talking with Hank. He held a white binder.

"Yeah?" Jessa asked. "Did you find out why?"

"No, and I have to." Nate said, determined. "It might be worse than I thought. See that binder my dad is carrying? Well, it was open earlier and I saw my name in it. He slammed it shut and told me to stay out of his business."

"That's probably exactly what you should do." Jessa told him. "Didn't you just figure out earlier this summer that you should be respecting your dad's authority?"

"But this is about me!" Nate said, raising his voice, then nervously glancing at Jay. Jay gave him an odd look. Nate stayed in his crouched pose and feigned an easy-going salute, until Jay turned away again.

"I have to see what's in that binder, Jessa. What if they're getting a divorce? Or declaring bankruptcy? Or sending me to boarding school? I have to find out and I need you to help me."

"Oh, let's see." Jessa pretended to be thinking. "No."

"You have to, it's really important!"

"It's snooping in your dad's private papers and I'm

not doing that. Forget it." Jessa said.

"Your name is in there, too." Nate said. Jessa blinked.

"I'm in your dad's binder? Why?"

"I have no idea." Nate hissed. "Just help me. You don't even have to look in it. You wouldn't be doing anything wrong, just accompanying me on an evening stroll. We won't break any camp rules. I'll do the dirty work, I just need you to be my wingman."

"Nate, I don't know about this." Jessa said. "What if my guess earlier was right and it's about your sixteenth birthday? Maybe I'm on the guest list, and that's in the binder. If we look it will wreck the surprise."

"I don't think that's it. I just have a bad feeling about this." Nate said darkly. "Come on. Do this for me. As an early birthday present."

Jessa sighed. "If we got caught-"

"We won't!" Nate said jubilantly. "Okay. We need to see where my dad leaves the binder, then get a look inside."

"I still don't know…" Jessa said, but Nate was already up, grabbing her hand and pulling her towards the door.

"Quick! He just left and he's got the binder!" Nate said. "Come on!" Jessa let Nate pull her out of the chapel. The woods were already growing dark; the tree-shadows long and black. "He went towards the lodge."

"He's probably going to snack, just like everyone else." Jessa sighed. "I'm telling you I don't want to get mixed up in this, Nate."

"Aren't you the teensiest bit curious why my dad is going around with your name in a folder?" Nate said, challenging.

"Not really. I don't care in the slightest." Jessa fibbed, though her interest was indeed piqued. "Haven't you ever learned that its wrong to snoop in other people's stuff?"

"Come on! He went in the lodge!" Nate said, pulling her faster.

"Big surprise. Snack is in there." Jessa said sarcastically. Nate jerked her behind a tree and peeked inside the lodge window.

"Alright, he's eating a brownie....Okay he's drinking orange juice; we have orange juice going down the hatch…" Nate reported.

"This is ridiculous, Nate! I want a brownie." Jessa turned to walk into the lodge but Nate grabbed her arm.

"Wait. He's turning. He's coming out. We can't leave now, it will blow our cover. I'm begging you." Nate said. "Okay, he's going to the parking lot. Let's go." Nate crept along the shadowed tree-line, walking on the grass to avoid crunching the mulched-path. Jessa followed closely behind, holding onto the back of Nate's hooded sweater for guidance in the dark. He stopped abruptly, and whirled around a tree, pulling her with him.

"Okay, he's unlocking the truck." Nate said, peering through the branches. The truck's interior light illuminated Fred's face as he tossed the binder onto the passenger seat and rifled through the glove-compartment.

"Get down, get down!" Nate hissed and put both hands on her shoulders, pushing her down to the ground, out of sight. Fred slammed the truck door closed was staring straight towards them.

Jessa barely breathed as Fred took a step in their direction, squinting in the darkness. Neither she nor Nate moved a muscle. Jessa realized that if he caught them like this; it would look bad. Really bad. It was bad enough to be sneaking around in the dark; but Nate's arms were practically around her. Still, she didn't dare move to shrug him off in case Fred heard the noise.

Finally, Fred turned on his heel and strode back to the lodge. When he was a good distance away, Jessa breathed a sigh of relief. Nate stood up and wiped his forehead. "Thank God." He mumbled. "Shoot, he locked the binder in the truck. I wonder if I can convince him to lend me the keys."

Just then, a twig snapped behind them and Jessa jumped, ready to dash. Standing in the shadowy woods several feet away was a dark figure; wearing a cowboy hat and slicker, watching them silently.

"Is that you Barb?" Nate called, stiltedly. "You scared us." Barb didn't respond. It was impossible to see her face. "You're not going to say anything about this, are you Barb?" Nate asked nervously, putting more distance between himself and Jessa. "We didn't do anything wrong. Honestly. It just looks bad. I-" Nate was cut off as Barb spoke.

In the darkness webs of lies
Spins deceits in youthful guise
All things shall be brought to light
Truth shall set man free tonight
Though of pure intent he be
To pry will cause him misery
Justice will prevail at last
Silence shall remain steadfast.

A car rumbled into the parking lot, its headlights blinding Jessa and Nate temporarily. Jessa shielded her eyes, trying to see who would be arriving at camp so late.

"Hey, where did she go?" Nate said, pointing to the place Barb had stood. There was no one there. Jessa looked back towards the parking lot, where someone was getting out of an old station wagon.

"Get back!" She hissed at Nate, pulling him behind the cover of the tree again. "Is that...?"

"What?" Nate whispered, his breath hot on her ear. Then, they both hear a loud, unmistakable laugh. Turning to each other at the exact same moment, Nate and Jessa mouthed, "Tiff?"

Jessa waited a while before returning to her lodge room. When she did, Tiff was just out of the shower and was towelling off her black hair. She wore flannel pyjamas and looked perky.

"Well hey there Jessa!" Tiff said, combing her hair and starting to braid it tightly. "How was your evening?"

"Oh, fine, fine." Jessa said airily. "And what may I ask did you get up to?"

"Chapel, of course." Tiff said. "I loved your singing."

Jessa grew white-hot. Was Tiff so willing to lie right to her face?

"Tiff, I don't appreciate it when you aren't honest with me." Jessa said tightly, her fists clenched. Confrontation wasn't Jessa's strongest point but she couldn't let this go. "I know you weren't at chapel."

"Was so!" Tiff said defensively, her dark brows drawing together.

"Are you going to claim you were at snack, too? Because I didn't see you there, either." Jessa put in. Tiff finished one black braid and tied it ferociously, then moved on to the next one.

"I felt sick. I needed some air." Tiff said, turning to the mirror.

"By air, do you mean the air in my brother's car?" Jessa said. She saw red splotches appear on the back of Tiff's neck. Tiff seemed to be thinking fast.

"Yes. Clark's car." Tiff whirled back around to face her. "I felt sick, so I slipped out halfway through chapel. Clark took me in to Sun Valley to get some medicine. Okay?"

"No. It's not okay." Jessa said. "You know it's against the rules to leave campus without authorization."

"For heaven's sake, Jessa, you really need to get a boyfriend." Tiff said, laughing stiffly. "You should see yourself right now. You're acting like my mother!"

"Maybe I just don't appreciate being lied to by my so-called 'best friend'!"

"I didn't lie!" Tiff insisted.

"Well you didn't exactly tell the whole truth, either,

now did you?" Jessa demanded.

"You know what Jessa? I don't appreciate that you were obviously spying on me. You must have been sneaking around like a detective to figure all this out. It's wrong to snoop you know. Want to talk about that?" Tiff asked. Jessa didn't answer. She couldn't admit that she and Nate had been sneaking around, holding hands in the dark, trying to look at his dad's private papers.

"No." Jessa said defiantly, too late. Triumph flashed in her eyes.

"Aha!" She pointed at Jessa. "There's no point trying to pretend you're as pure as the driven snow, Jessa. We all have our vices. Mine is true love. You should be happy for me; I'm finally over Wade."

"Ugh." Jessa flopped herself down on her bed, miserably. "Look, I don't want to fight anymore. Agreed?"

"You got it." Tiff said, pulling on socks. "What are best friends for?" Jessa didn't respond. She changed into her pyjamas, too, and climbed into bed. Marsha came in a few minutes later. When Marsha took her toothbrush to the bathroom, leaving Jessa and Tiff alone again, Tiff spoke up.

"Jessa?"

'What?" Jessa said shortly.

"Do you think, I could maybe, possibly, well, would you mind if I maybe-"

"Just say it, Tiff." Jessa sighed.

"I want to move to your house. After camp's over."

Jessa didn't respond. Her immediate urge was to yell 'NOOOO!' at the top of her lungs. Instead she clicked off the lamp and said nothing. Tiff continued doggedly.

"You see, my parents work a lot, and my sister's at college, and it's just really lonely at my house. If you could convince your parents that I can stay at your place-"

"I don't think that's a good idea, Tiff." Jessa cut her off wearily.

"You haven't even heard my plan yet." Tiff sounded

hurt.

"Fine."

"I can live down in the guest room, and pay rent and everything. I bet your parents will say yes. They are so sweet and welcoming. We'll get to see each other every day. It will be so fun. It will be like camp never ended. What do you think?" Tiff sounded so desperate, so hopeful.

"It's not up to me, Tiff." Jessa said. "It's up to my parents. It's their house. I don't think they'll go for it."

"But you can ask them, right?" Tiff asked. "If you convince-"

"I don't feel comfortable with this Tiff."

"Just think about it, will you?" Tiff rolled over in bed. "You can tell me your answer in a couple days." Marsha slipped back in and settled into bed.

Fine. I'll tell you in a couple days. And I already know what my answer will be. Jessa thought to herself as she drifted off to sleep.

Just before she was fully asleep, it occurred to Jessa that Tiff had claimed Clark took her to the drugstore, because she felt sick. But how could Clark have known Tiff was suddenly sick? Tiff had been just fine at dinner, Jessa remembered. She would have had to call Clark to come get her. Why not go to the camp nurse, instead?

Jessa felt funny about the whole business. She didn't want to believe Tiff was stretching the truth. Yet, she didn't know what else to believe.

CHAPTER 7
FASHION ADVICE

The next morning, Jessa stopped by the staff lounge on her way to breakfast. She saw there was a letter in her mailbox again. It looked exactly like the letter she had received on Sunday; a plain white envelope with her name scrawled across the front. Tearing it open, Jessa scanned it, again searching for a clue of who it could be from. Again, it was unsigned.

Jessa,

I was reading my bible and came across a passage that made me think of you. It's Philippians 1:3. It's actually Paul referring to the church in Phillipa, and he says; 'I thank God when I think of you.' Well, I may be out of context here, but when I read that, I thought of you.

As you go about your day, be encouraged and remember that God loves you and he is in control. And know also that you are special. Have a wonderful day.

Sincerely Yours.

Jessa exhaled slowly. She hadn't realized she had been holding her breath while she read. She folded the letter and retraced her steps to her room, tucking the letter into her journal. The letter seemed so sincere. She didn't think Patrick would have had the capacity to write something like that. But what about his hero comment the other day, that had made her wonder if he wrote the first one?

Jessa hurried down the stairs and ended up at the back of the breakfast line, behind Russ and Jay. They were teasing each other about something and mock-wrestling against the wall.

"Hey, hey, break it up, folks." Jessa said jovially. "I'm sure this can be worked out diplomatically."

"But Jessa, Jay said I have to eat the mystery egg-surprise." Russ pouted and hung his head dramatically.

"When your girlfriend cooks it, you have to eat it." Jay said. "Right Jessa?"

"Sure. Yes! Of course you do." She fixed Russ with a steely glare, her nose in the air. "You will eat it and like it!" Russ stepped forward and penitently held out his plate to Cory-Lynn.

"Oh, fairest maiden of sunshine and flowers," Russ monologue, "Permit me to compliment thy wonderful egg supreme delight-"

"Wrap it up buddy." Jay elbowed Russ out of the way. "Some of us actually want the egg surprise while its still hot." Feigning offence, Russ kissed Cory-Lynn's hand lingeringly, while Jay poked him in the back. "Move along, move along." Jay turned to Jessa and rolled his eyes. "Can you believe this guy?"

"Just one scoop, please." Jessa smiled, holding out her plate to Cory-Lynn.

"How's your morning going so far?" Jay asked, passing her some cutlery.

"It's fine. Things have been interesting lately." Jessa said, grabbing a napkin.

"How?" Jay asked.

"Well..." Jessa followed Jay to the dining room and looked over at the wrangler table. It appeared that Nate was timing Patrick to see how fast he could finish a full plate of eggs. Tiff and Marsha were cheering him on, while slobbery flecks of egg dribbled over the table. Wade was deep in conversation with Hank while Barb listened intently. Grimacing, Jessa braced herself. "I'll tell you about it later." Jessa promised. "Oh, hey, how's Kenny doing by the way?"

"That kid is awesome." Jay smiled. "And he thinks you're the best sister since sliced bread."

"He's not wrong." Jessa chuckled. "Just watch that he doesn't try on your shoes and go tap-dancing around in them, wearing just his underwear."

"What?" Jay looked bemused.

"Don't ask." Jessa grinned. "Okay, see you at worship practice." Steeling herself, Jessa headed over to the table.

"Well if it isn't Princess Charming." Patrick said loudly as she approached. A blob of egg clung to his chin.

"Morning." Wade stood and pulled out a chair for her. "Allow me."

"Thank you, Wade." Jessa said. Despite her doubts she thrilled at his attention and rewarded him with a sweet smile. He tipped his hat to her and winked in reply.

"So Jessa, are you gonna be my date to the banquet or what?" Patrick said loudly.

"Patrick…" Jessa groaned, her patience already thinning.

"Come on. I clean up real nice; you'll be shocked." Patrick cajoled, reaching over and grabbing her shoulder. Jessa flinched and wriggled out of his meaty grasp.

"Don't." She warned, giving him an icy glare.

"Fine, fine, I get it." Patrick threw his hands up in surrender. "The ice-queen wants to play hard to get. What does a guy have to do? Flowers? Candy? Love sonnet? What's it gonna take to get you off your high horse?"

"Hey, now." Wade interjected firmly. "Knock it off, Patrick."

"Why should I?" Patrick turned to Wade, his beady eyes glittering. "You gonna make me, cowboy?"

"Is there a problem here?" Hank said, tuning into the conversation. Wade and Patrick were glaring at each other.

"No, Hank. No problem." Wade said after a weighted pause, his blue eyes still fixed on Patrick's.

"Whatever." Patrick pushed back his chair and loafed away, leaving a mess of eggs and napkin littering the table.

"Whoa." Marsha said, sitting back.

"Aw, Patrick's just joking around." Tiff brushed it off. "He's always like that."

"Hey." Jessa leaned towards Wade and lowered her voice. "Thanks."

"You're welcome." Wade said, smiling. "It looked like you needed a little help, there."

"You have no idea." Jessa said wearily. "I feel like I need a body-guard around that guy." Wade cocked his head thoughtfully.

"How about if I walk you over to worship practice after this, then? It's on my way to the barn, anyway. I'll make sure he doesn't bother you." Jessa considered for a minute, looking into Wade's eyes.

"Well, sure." She finally agreed. "You're on."

Worship practice took longer than usual. By the time it finished, there was only about half an hour left before lunch; not quite enough time to bother going down to the barn. Jessa decided to go for a stroll. It was gorgeously sunny outside, with a gentle breeze scattering some early-fallen leaves.

"I'm going for a walk." She announced to the band. "Anyone care to join me?"

"Can't." Russ shook his head, tucking his bass into its case. "I have a very important phone call to make."

"Sure." Jay said, propping his guitar into its stand. "Let's go." He led the way and held the chapel door open for her. "Where do you want to walk?"

"How about down to the creek?" Jessa suggested, breathing in the fresh air as she stepped outside.

"Sure." Jay said. "As long as we're back in time for lunch. My cabin's depending on me."

They walked slowly, savouring the late-morning sun. For a while they didn't say anything at all. Jessa enjoyed the comfortable quiet; which was punctuated by the crunch of the path under their feet, and the birds singing in the trees. As they approached the creek, Jay spoke.

"You said you were having a weird morning?"

"Oh. Yeah." Jessa said sheepishly. "A weird week, actually. Or, weird summer."

"How so?" Jay asked lightly. He was wearing flip-flop sandals, Jessa noticed, and board-shorts with a Hawaiian print t-shirt. She had grown accustomed to his bold looks and hardly noticed anymore.

"It's just been a lot more drama and love triangles than I expected." Jessa sighed with a little smile. "I guess that's just part of being a teenager, right?"

"I guess." Jay shrugged. "It's like that at bible college too, though."

"Really?"

"Oh yeah." Jay grinned. "Worse. Everyone's trying to find Mr. or Mrs. Right, pronto."

"Sounds like a fun time." Jessa laughed.

"It is fun." Jay conceded. "Russ has been awesome as a roommate. Hopefully things don't get super awkward this year, though, if he's hanging out with Cory-Lynn twenty-four-seven. And don't get me wrong," Jay quickly clarified. "I love Cory-Lynn. She's a sweetheart and they are great together. It's just that I know it will be different now that he's in love."

"Is Russ really in love?" Jessa asked, stopping at the edge of the creek and looking out over the water. "He's only known her a couple months."

"I think so." Jay nodded, picking up a rock and trying to skip it. It sank immediately.

"Epic fail." Jessa teased. Jay grinned and picked up another.

"Hey come on, at least I tried. Let's see you skip one." Jessa picked up a flat stone and whipped it across the water. It skipped four times then sank. She looked expectantly at Jay.

"I concede; you're the winner. You rock." The corner of Jay's mouth twitched. "No pun intended."

"Good grief." Jessa pretended to be exasperated. She turned back towards camp and gestured that they should walk back. He fell into step beside her. "So, Jay, tell me, have you ever been in love?"

Jay looked at her quickly, a surprised look in his eyes. "Why do you ask?"

"Well, you seem to be an expert on the subject of Russ and Cory-Lynn's love. Plus earlier this summer, you were giving me advice about holding out for true love. Have you ever had a girlfriend before?"

"A girlfriend? No, not really." Jay said, starting the climb up the sloping hill away from the creek. "But have I been in love? Yes, I would say I have."

"Do you want to have a girlfriend, someday? I mean, to have what Russ and Cory-Lynn have." Jessa clarified. She was wondering if she knew anyone at her church she could set him up with. He was such a nice guy. Maybe Eva, who played piano sometimes.

"Sure, if it was the right girl." Jay said. "It would have to be someone pretty special."

"You know," Jessa said thoughtfully, looking him up and down slyly. "You might have a little more luck getting a girlfriend if you did something about those dreadlocks."

"These?" Jay grabbed one and held it up, appraising it. "What's wrong with these puppies?" Jessa burst out laughing. Jay looked genuinely perplexed. "They're not that bad, are they?"

"Well," Jessa giggled, "Not every girl would appreciate, I mean, if you were to say…"

"What?" Jay said.

"Chop them off?"

"They can hear you! You're hurting their feelings!" Jay exclaimed, his eyes twinkling as he cradled a few dreadlocks lovingly.

"Sorry." Jessa tried to suppress her smile as they approached the dining hall. The lunch bell rang just as they entered. "And say, if you were to dress in more normal clothes…"

"Normal?" Jay looked down at his bold outfit. "Hey, I'll have you know that the ladies appreciate a bright, beachy-look!"

"Oh, is that what you're going for?" Jessa said mercilessly. "I couldn't tell if you were going for Jamaican pirate, or homeless skater. Look, I'm just saying this to help you out. You know, so you can get a girlfriend one day."

She headed towards the ladies room to wash up, waving goodbye to Jay. He clutched his hand over his heart, pretending to be mortally wounded, though he was still grinning. Chuckling, Jessa breezed into the bathroom.

That afternoon, Jessa had two lovely trail rides on Fairlight; first leading, then flanking one for Marsha. After that she and Wade taught horse-care class together. Wade was kind and attentive. Jessa even flirted back a little, trying to ignite some of the same feelings she had had for him earlier in the summer. It was fun, but felt a little silly, too.

As they walked back to dinner, Nate pulled her aside and said he still hadn't found out his dad's big secret, and now the binder seemed to have vanished.

"It's just as well, Nate." Jessa told him, striding along beside him. "You know it's wrong to mess around with his stuff anyway. I can't believe I let you drag me along on your first attempt."

"I'm telling you, I think it's bad." Nate said.

"When did you get to be such a dooms-day, glass half-empty sort?" Jessa quizzed. "What happened to the happy-go-lucky, easy-going Nate? Where is he and what did you do with him?"

"Ha-ha." Nate said robotically.

"Look, just go have a talk with your dad, man to man, and see if he'll tell you. If he won't you should drop it." Jessa said.

"Fine." Nate said, setting his jaw. "Oh, by the way, I did talk to my dad last night about something else. I asked if I could take you as my date to the formal banquet on Saturday."

"You did?" Jessa felt blind-sighted.

"Sure. Just as friends, obviously. But he said 'No, you're not sixteen yet.' Can you believe that?" Nate whined.

"Wow." Jessa said, breathing easier.

"I know." Nate huffed. "My birthday is in like, three weeks. He said I can go to the banquet with a group but not with an official date. Talk about a stickler."

"Yeah." Jessa scanned the skies, noticing dark clouds forming overhead. "Still, I'm flattered you wanted to ask me. As friends, of course. I really enjoy being just friends with you. Anyway." Jessa cleared her throat, realizing she had been rambling. "The main thing is to respect your dad right? Before you know it you'll be grown up and out of the nest, and then you can do whatever you want."

"I guess." Nate said gloomily, just as the first raindrops fell.

After chapel that evening, Jessa sprinted back to the lodge with Marsha, holding her sweater over her head and dodging puddles. A thunder-storm had struck during dinner and was still raging hours later. She was soaked by the time she reached the lodge.

"I could use a hot shower." Marsha said, shivering.

"I'm pretty stiff. I tried riding Polka-dot today and he threw a total hissy fit. Bucked me off."

"Really?" Jessa said.

"Yeah." Marsha said. "And he wouldn't even let Nate near him. Freaked out."

"That's too bad." Jessa said. "I did wonder if Tiff was too hard on him. Hank didn't stop her though."

"I guess maybe that approach works on some horses. A lot of cowboys do it that way." Marsha shrugged. "Let's get our stuff." They sprinted up the stairs to grab towels and shampoo, then dashed to the staff washroom and claimed shower stalls. Jessa stepped under the hot water, feeling it instantly warm her up.

"Oh, hey." Marsha called from her stall, her voice echoing off the tile wall. "Did you decide if you're going to the banquet with Wade?"

"I don't know yet." Jessa called back, scrubbing shampoo into her long hair. "Do you think I should?"

"Yes." Marsha said firmly. "Why are you holding back from him?"

"Something just doesn't feel quite right." Jessa said, rinsing her head. "Maybe I'm just still sore that he picked Virginia over me. I don't want to be anyone's second choice."

"I don't know if you are." Marsha's voice reverberated. "I mean, didn't you kind of turn him down, right before Virginia came? Maybe you were his first choice but he gave up hope."

"Maybe."

"You should just talk to him about it. Get it all out in the open." Marsha called.

"Maybe." Jessa repeated, turning off the water and grabbing her towel. "Oh, and I got another letter from the mystery man this morning."

"What! How could you not tell me?" Marsha squealed.

"I'll show you." Jessa said, changing into pyjamas.

Back in their room, Marsha read the new letter thoughtfully.

"Hmm." She said. "I agree it's definitely not from Patrick. I mean, no offence, but I don't think his brain even works this way, you know? It's gotta be Wade."

"Maybe it's from Nate." Jessa said quietly. She had had growing suspicions since the walk back from the barn.

"Nate?" Marsha's eyes widened. "Why would you think that?" Jessa squirmed awkwardly.

"He said he wanted to ask me to the banquet, but his dad said no." Jessa mumbled. "And earlier this week, he sort of held my hand in the woods when we were following his dad."

"I can't believe this!" Marsha roared incredulously. "How could I not see this?"

"Look, it's probably nothing." Jessa said. "He even said he just meant it as a friend. I'm just reading too much into it."

"Honestly, Jessa, is there a guy at this camp that isn't in love with you?" Marsha teased.

"Marsha..." Jessa collapsed on her bed. "It's not easy being me."

"You're so lucky." Marsha quipped. "And the fact that all these guys are taller than you is just a bonus. You have your pick of the litter. Nate, Wade, or Patrick. That's all three of the male wranglers."

"You make it sound like I'm on a game show."

"The question is, which one do you want?" Marsha asked, playing along with her best tv-hostess voice.

"Wait a minute." Jessa said, sitting up suddenly. "Where's Tiff?" Marsha looked towards bed. It was empty and perfectly made up.

"You know, I didn't see her at chapel tonight." Marsha said. "Or at dinner, for that matter. I wonder where she is?"

"I bet I can guess." Jessa said, scowling. "I wonder what her big excuse will be this time for sneaking off with my brother?"

"We shouldn't jump to conclusions." Marsha said, striding to the window and looking out. "She could be doing any number of things. Let's give her the benefit of the doubt."

CHAPTER 8
BUY ME A DREAM

The next morning after breakfast, Jessa gave her parents a quick phone call before worship practice. Her dad answered.

"How's our girl?" Eugene said. Jessa sat on the couch in the staff lounge, cradling the phone to her ear.

"I'm fine, dad." Jessa said. "How are you and mom, and Clark?"

"We are all good." Eugene said. "How's camp?"

"It's okay." Jessa said, twisting the long phone cord around her fingers. "I can't believe it's the last week though. It's going to be really hard to leave Fairlight."

"You really care about that horse, don't you?" Her dad asked. Jessa could picture him, sitting at his home office and leaning back in his leather desk chair.

"Yeah." Jessa said. "I've trained her myself and got her to be so good. Now I'll leave her and she'll be wrecked."

"You could just buy her." Her dad suggested. "There's plenty of room for a horse on the acreage."

"You'd really let me do that?" Jessa said, fiddling with

the end of her long pony-tail. She hadn't considered the possibility of buying Fairlight.

"As long as you use your own money. And you would have to be the one to take care of her." Eugene stipulated. "You'd be buying her hay, and paying vet and farrier bills. You'd probably need to get a job to do all that."

"I do have some savings already." Jessa reminded him. "From all the babysitting I did last winter."

"Well, if you're sure that's what you want to do, talk to Hank about it." Eugene said. "It's your decision, but your mom and I will support you if you decide it's what you really want."

"Okay." Jessa said. "Oh, and dad? Tiff asked me if she can move in."

"Yes, Tiff mentioned that to me last night." Her dad said. "She said you seemed onboard with it."

"I'm not!" Jessa said quickly. "I told Tiff it wasn't a good idea."

"Well, I told her flat-out no." Eugene said comfortably. "I'm not in the business of becoming a youth hostel for your brother's various girlfriends." Jessa breathed a sigh of relief, then chuckled.

"I can't believe she had the guts to ask you to move in." Jessa said. "How did she take it when you said no?"

"She didn't say much." Eugene said. "I think she was surprised. I get the feeling she's used to getting her way."

"She is." Jessa said, looking at the clock. Worship practice was starting soon. Suddenly something clicked into place. "Wait a minute dad. Are you saying you talked to Tiff last night?"

"Well, she and Clark stopped by here on the way to the concert."

"Tiff went to a concert with Clark last night?" Jessa said, irritably. "I can't believe this. So that's where she was. She still wasn't back when Marsha and I fell asleep, and today she slept through breakfast. She's breaking curfew and sneaking around."

"That's her problem." Eugene said casually. "Clark isn't breaking any of our rules; he's been quite forthcoming and open with us."

"It makes things awkward for me." Jessa said, clenching her teeth. "It's like I'm expected to cover for her."

"You aren't." Eugene reminded her. "If she's causing trouble and sneaking around, that's up to her. You don't need to make things easier for her, even if you are best friends."

"We aren't." Jessa frowned. "I gotta go, Dad, I have worship practice."

"Okay, Hun. Have a good day. Love you." He clicked off and Jessa jogged to the chapel, her mind racing.

Jessa didn't see Tiff until lunch time, and by then she was seething. Tiff, however, seemed to be avoiding her gaze. Towards the end of the meal, Jessa leaned over.

"Can we talk?" Jessa said. "It's important."

"I can't." Tiff said, rising from the table. "I have a previous engagement."

"You're leaving?" Jessa asked, standing as well.

"Dentist appointment. I cleared it with Hank." Tiff shrugged and started towards the door. Jessa followed her, talking quietly.

"By dentist appointment, do you mean sneaking off with my brother again?"

"Would you cool it?" Tiff scowled, tossing her stiff black braids over her shoulders and placing her hand on the door. "Your brother was kind enough to offer me a ride to the dentist. What's the big deal?"

"Now you're skiving off work to go off on dates." Jessa shook her head. "I can't believe you."

"Have you ever had a crown come loose?" Tiff demanded. "It's horrible. And speaking of skiving off work, how's worship practice been going? I bet it's real nice to skip out on the morning chores to sing a couple songs. Now back off and let me go."

"No!" Jessa blocked the door. "I don't want you going out with my brother anymore, Tiff. And by the way we're not best friends." She shot out before she could stop herself. A hurt look rippled across Tiff's face, but was quickly replaced with a hard frown.

"Maybe it's not up to you if I date him." She growled. "I'm going out with him whether you like it or not. So you may as well get used to the idea. Now get out of my way." Tiff pushed past Jessa and stormed to the parking lot.

Jessa rode flank for both trail rides that afternoon, with Wade leading. Jessa wondered if she had been too harsh in her conversation with Tiff earlier; after all maybe Jessa was over-reacting.

Bending down to ruffle Fairlight's mane, Jessa sighed irritably, and looked ahead. There were twelve campers slouched on their horses, and Wade's broad shoulders swayed slightly with Bea's steps at the front. He rode with such calm ease, like he had been born in the saddle. Of course he had grown up on a ranch, and probably had been riding before he could walk.

She thought back to what her dad had said, that she could offer to buy Fairlight. She had watched the campers excitedly yanking on the trail-horses reins all summer, and kicking, and yelling whoa indiscriminately. Jessa made up her mind to ask Hank about it right after the ride.

As soon as the campers had tied up their horses and raced up for tuck, Jessa went looking for her boss. He was in the office with Marsha and Barb.

"Hank, can I speak to you?" Jessa asked, her hands trembling slightly.

"Sure. Let's hear it." Hank said, crossing his arms and

leaning back on the counter's edge. Jessa glanced at Marsha and Barb.

"Hank, I want to buy Fairlight." Jessa announced with gusto, expecting Hank to jump at the idea. Instead, his look went from inquisitive to solemn. Marsha slipped out of the office.

"She's not for sale, Jessa." Hank said, adjusting his cowboy hat. Barb's expression was unreadable.

"I heard you say earlier this summer that any horse is for sale, if it's the right price." Jessa argued. Hank considered this for a moment and stroked his beard.

"What are you offering?" He asked. Jessa made her offer, listing the entire sum of her savings account. She was proud of the amount. But Hank shook his head.

"I'm afraid not, Jessa." Hank said. "Fairlight's a registered Morgan, and a buckskin, at that. That's rare. Plus you won't find such a nice temperament on any old horse. She's worth double that, at least. Even then I don't know if I could let her go. She's such a great horse."

His words fell like a gavel, smashing her hopes. Jessa felt stunned. She had been so sure Hank would accept her offer.

"I see." Jessa said, tears suddenly threatening.

"I'm sorry, Jessa." Hank said, a softer look in his eyes. "I have to think of what's best for the camp, from a business stand-point."

Jessa nodded, unable to speak. She knew there was absolutely no way she could afford that price. Backing away, she pushed open the office door. "Fine, I understand." She whispered shakily and fled.

Jessa raced out the barn door and onto the porch. She didn't even know where she was going. She ran around the corner of the barn and almost right into Wade.

"Whoa!" Wade caught her in his arms and held her steady, looking into her eyes. "Hey, are you alright?" Jessa couldn't help it. She burst into tears, her eyes involuntarily squeezing shut. Vaguely she felt Wade put his arms around her and lead her to the bench under the porch.

CHAPTER 9
CALM BEFORE THE STORM

Jessa calmed eventually, and told Wade what had happened. He didn't say much but stayed beside her, his arm around her shoulders. When she finally dried her eyes on her sleeve, she started to feel somewhat silly. She had had a melt-down like a toddler.

"Sorry." Jessa sniffed. "I guess it's all catching up with me."

"It's all good." Wade assured her. He smelled like clover. Jessa realized she had never been this close to Wade before; she was basically in his arms. Part of her felt shy and awkward; but another part felt cared-for and comforted. His strong arm around her shoulders was warm and secure; making her feel protected. So why did she want to run away?

Finally, Jessa looked up into Wade's face. Wade was looking back at her intently, a soft look in his eyes. Feeling increasingly uncomfortable, Jessa eased out from under his arm and stood.

"I should go." Jessa said, looking down. "I need to unsaddle Fairlight before dinner."

"Wait." Wade said huskily, standing and stepping closer again. "Don't go, Jessa."

"Wade, I can't do this. I don't think I can be here with you, like this." Jessa clasped her hands together awkwardly, looking away.

"Don't keep running away from me, Jessa." Wade said gently. "Please. Give us a chance."

"I don't know if I can." Jessa whispered, fidgeting. "I mean, I used to, of course. I still sometimes, I wonder if-" Jessa stopped, realizing she wasn't making any sense. She looked up into his handsome face. She took a deep breath and tried again.

"Wade, I really liked you for most of the summer. But I have to be honest." She said miserably, looking away again. "I was really hurt when you dropped me, back when Virginia was here. It was like I didn't even exist anymore. I don't want to be your second choice."

"Is that what you think?" Wade said softly. "That you were my second choice?" Jessa nodded miserably, kicking a piece of straw with her cowboy boot.

"Jessa, that wasn't it at all." Wade sighed and took off his cowboy hat, raking his hand through his caramel-coloured hair. "Remember back when we first met? I told you I liked you and wanted to ask you out?" Jessa nodded. "Well, you turned me down, right? You said you wanted to be just friends."

"Well, yes." Jessa reluctantly agreed. "I thought we should be friends at the time; but I didn't mean it was necessarily over between us."

"But I didn't know that." Wade interjected gently. "I thought you were rejecting me, in a nice way. So when Virginia was here, I tried to get my mind off you by hanging out with her. She was the second choice, not you."

"Oh." Jessa said, confused.

"After Virginia left, Marsha told me to try again. But I didn't know if you had any feelings left for me. I still don't know." Wade smiled, his dimples showing.

"I think I might." Jessa said, feeling numb inside. "I don't know what I feel anymore. I'm so confused."

"Well, I still like you, Jessa." Wade said plainly. "I feel like somehow we missed our chance or something, you know?" He looped his thumbs through his belt-loops and leaned back against a post. "But maybe we can still have a chance. To be together. As a couple."

Jessa felt dizzy. Wade was finally saying what she had dreamed he would say for most of the summer; yet now she didn't know what to do with it.

"But the summer's over." Jessa blurted. Wade nodded, exhaling.

"We could see each other on the weekends. My dad's ranch is only a few hours away." Wade suggested hopefully.

"I don't know." Jessa buried her head in her hands. "This is all so fast. Doesn't it feel like something is missing to you?"

"Missing?" Wade frowned, looking around. "What do you mean?"

"I don't know." Jessa repeated wretchedly, massaging her eyebrows.

"Will you at least think about it? Us?" Wade asked. "And let me know in the next couple days?"

Jessa took a deep breath and nodded. "I'll let you know as soon as I can." She promised.

That evening after chapel, Jessa sprawled on her bed to journal. Her feelings were all so jumbled she wanted to get them on paper, raw and unfiltered, before she vented them on Marsha later.

August 25th

I trained Fairlight myself. I am a volunteer here. I gave up my entire summer for no pay. And what thanks do I get? Nothing.

Fairlight will be ruined. She will be heartbroken and think I abandoned her, and never reach the potential she could have if she were mine. Hank is being unreasonable. He himself has been the one to brag about the amazing connection I have with Fairlight, and how a horse and rider may only have that once in a lifetime. How could he do this to me? It's not like that amount of money means anything to a camp this size. It's a drop in the bucket. I don't deserve this! Neither does Fairlight!

Where does he think I can come up with that much money? I'm a high school student. Maybe if I was working at a paid job; which I well could have done this summer. But no. Here I am volunteering for FREE at this camp. Clearly there is no gratitude for that. Well I'll tell you who WON'T be coming back here next summer, thank you very much.

Everything's a disaster. Wade finally admitted he wants to date me, but there's only three days left of camp. Plus, I don't know if I want that anymore. Some moments I think 'he's probably the one!' and other moments I feel uncomfortable around him. Earlier today he had his arm around me and was looking into my eyes, and it felt wrong and awkward, and I wanted to step back and put space between us. I didn't like him so close to my face.

Patrick is being a total jerk, and most days I feel like throttling his chubby neck. If he makes one more comment about my hormones I may punch him in the face.

Oh, and I had a nice fight with Tiff and told her to stay away from Clark. She keeps sneaking off with him and expecting me to cover for her. Now she's even skipping out on her barn duties. I'm sick of it.

After chapel ended I stayed a while and told Jay what was going on with Tiff. He could tell something was bothering me. He suggested maybe I should talk to my brother about it, and tell him how I'm feeling. I told him that Clark and I have a hot-and-cold relationship; but he said it doesn't matter; he's your brother and if it bothers you this much, you should be honest with him. Friends come and go, but family is forever.

The only thing that keeps me going is Fairlight. I have three more days with her; then after the staff banquet, I have to leave her

and go on with my life. I don't know how I will ever be able to say goodbye.
Jessa Davies.

As Jessa closed her journal, Tiff flounced into the room. She had been away the entire afternoon and evening.

"Hey, girl!" Tiff beamed, as though there had been no fight earlier. "Journaling? Good idea, I need to update mine, too."

Jessa clenched her jaw shut to keep from saying something she would regret, though she was tempted to say, *And how was the dentist? Must have been quite the ordeal to be in the dentist's chair for six hours!* Instead Jessa stood and marched out of the room, to the staff lounge. Jay, Russ, and Cory-Lynn were there already, sprawled on the couch playing a game of cards.

"Hey, Jessa." Jay said, smiling up at her. "You want to hang out?" He motioned to the cards.

"No thanks." Jessa smiled tightly back. "I decided to take your advice and call my brother."

"Good idea." Jay praised. "Want us to step out?"

"Um, maybe if you don't mind." Jay stood up and stretched.

"Come on, you love birds." He said to Russ and Cory-Lynn. "I have to get back to my cabin anyway. I told Erik I'd come back after snack. Hopefully they haven't torn the place down by now."

"Tell Kenny I said hi." Jessa called after them as they left.

"Will do." Jay waved. "Sleep well, Jess!"

Jessa scooped up the phone and dialled her home number. Her mom answered.

"Hey, Jess-Jess! How are you?" Nancy said.

"I'm good, mom." Jessa said. "I was wondering if Clark is there. I want to talk to him."

"Looks like he's just pulling into the driveway." Nancy said. Jessa could hear the dog barking in the background. "We have a minute til he gets in. So how is Kenny doing?"

"I think he's having fun." Jessa said, sitting on the edge of the couch. "Jay is a nice guy, so I'm sure he's in good hands."

"Yes." Nancy said slyly. "I was quite impressed with Jay. Seemed like an excellent young man indeed."

"Mother." Jessa rolled her eyes, fighting a smile.

"What?" Nancy said. "Since nothing seems to be happening with that Wade, you may as well-"

"Actually, things might still happen with Wade." Jessa contradicted.

"Oh, really?" Nancy said coyly. "Do tell."

"Mom, I just need to talk to Clark." Jessa begged. "We can talk boys when I get home on Saturday, okay?"

"Fine." Nancy sighed. "Jess-Jess doesn't want to tell ole' momma anything. Okay, here's Clark." There was a rustling noise, and then her brother's voice came on the line.

"Hey kid." Clark was over a year older. Jessa could picture him in the kitchen, tossing his keys on the counter and shrugging out of his leather jacket. She wondered if his recently pierced ear was still infected. Or if he had shaved off that ridiculous little Mohawk haircut. "What's up?"

"Clark." Jessa said, suddenly nervous. "I know it's none of my business, but I don't think you should go out with Tiff anymore." The other end of the line was silent. "Clark?"

"I heard ya, kiddo." Clark said. "And you'll be shocked to hear that I think you're right."

"Really?" Jessa had been prepared to convince him.

"Look, I hope this doesn't make things weird for you, because I know you and Tiff are friends." Clark said. "But I thought we were just having fun. You know, casually. But now she's starting to freak me out. She calls me all the time, all clingy. I even heard her ask dad if she could move in." Clark said, picking up steam. "I mean, that's freaky.

We've been going out a couple weeks, and she already wants to move in?" Clark chuckled.

"So, you're going to end it?" Jessa asked tentatively.

"Yep." Clark said. "I'll drive over there tomorrow and tell her it's over, in person."

"Okay, good." Jessa said. "She's breaking all these curfew rules and stuff, and keeps expecting me to cover for her."

"She is?" Clark sounded surprised. "I thought she had permission to be out late. She honestly didn't tell me, Jessa. Mom and dad knew what was going on the whole time, and they never had a problem with it."

"It's not your fault." Jessa sighed. "I just wish you'd never gone out with her in the first place."

"Hmm." Clark said. "I think the last straw for me was this evening. Kenny saw us in the parking lot, and she paid him twenty bucks not to tell anyone she had been out with me."

"She really did that?" Jessa gasped.

"Yep." Clark said. "Trying to bribe our little brother to lie? There's something twisted about that."

"Yeah." Jessa said. "Well, I guess I didn't need to call about this after all."

"It's all good." Clark said smoothly. "I'm thinking of asking out your friend Willa next. The blonde from youth group. Now, she's not crazy, is she?"

"Clark!" Jessa rolled her eyes. "Stop dating my friends!" Clark chortled.

"Okay fine, Willa can stay single for now. Gotta go, Jessa. Have a good night."

"Bye, Clark."

CHAPTER 10
HERE COMES THUNDER

Jessa avoided Wade's gaze at breakfast the next morning; not ready to make a decision about his proposition just yet. Towards the end of the meal, Patrick started attempting to burp the alphabet, and Jessa decided it was time to leave the table. She had a few minutes before worship practice started, and wanted to check her mail box before she walked over to the chapel.

She bounded up the stairs two at a time, feeling her high-pony tail swish and slap her between the shoulder-blades with each step. She peeked into the lounge and saw that, indeed, her mail slot had two envelopes in it.

Her pulse quickening, Jessa ripped open the first envelope.

Jessa

I know you are going through some hard stuff right now. Believe me, I wish you didn't have to! But sometimes God has a way of using these challenging experiences to help us grow stronger. It forces us to trust him more. Remember, "Give all your worries and cares to God, for he cares for you." That's from 1 Peter 5:7, the New Living Translation.

You don't have to go through all this alone. You have friends you can lean on, who care about you. But mostly, God knows what you are going through. He is right there with you and he knows what's best for you.

Life can be confusing sometimes, can't it? It can be hard to know which way to go. There are so many options; so many paths. I like to remember this verse: "Trust in the Lord with all of your heart, and lean not on your own understanding. In all your ways, acknowledge him, and he will make your paths straight." Proverbs 3:5.

We don't need to have it all figured out. We only need to trust that God is in control; and since he loves us, he will take care of our needs. The more we acknowledge that; the more clear our way forward will become.

Have a wonderful day, and know someone is cheering for you!

Sincerely yours.

Jessa stood frozen on the spot, the words hitting her heart, hard. She knew she needed to trust God more. After all, what had all her stressing accomplished? Nothing.

"I'm sorry." Jessa whispered aloud in the empty lounge. She strode to the window and looked out. She saw the pack of wranglers walking away as a group, towards the barn. Nate was elbowing Wade. Barb floated along beside Hank like a shadow, while Hank was talking animatedly with Patrick and Marsha. Tiff wasn't with them.

Lord, I want to trust you. Jessa prayed silently. *I feel like I'm running around like a crazy person lately, out of control. I need help. I need you to show me what path to take here. Do I date Wade? Or not?*

Jessa rested her elbows on the window sill, watching all the people leaving the building. Kenny skipped out with his friends, flanked by Erik. Ms. Sheila trotted in the direction of the office, staring at a clip-board and looking serious. Nate's dad, Fred, stalked that same way a few moments later, the white-clipboard tucked under his arm.

I know there is a time for everything, Lord. Maybe this is a season of good-byes, and of moving on from camp. But is that really what I'm supposed to do? Leave Fairlight here? I was so sure Hank would let me have her, but now it seems like I never can. It hurts. Jessa felt a calm presence come over her, as though God understood her sorrow and was comforting her. *Thank you for always being with me, Lord.*

Jessa looked at the second letter. It was also in a white envelope with her name on the front. Tearing it open, she read it quickly.

Jessa,

I'm really glad we had the conversation we did, and I know you'll give it some thought.

On another note; I hope you know you can trust me. I will do anything to win your heart. Just tell me what I need to do, and I will do it.

Will you do me an honour? Will you meet me tonight, right after chapel? We need to finish the conversation we started. Meet me right after chapel up at the front, near the fire-place.

I'll be waiting for you.

You know who. ;)

Looking at the anonymous letters, Jessa could see that two distinct people had written them. The writing was completely different; one was scrawling, and the other a bold, upright print. She couldn't recall what the writing looked like in the original letters. She would need to compare these new letters to the first two she had received to learn which ones were written by the same author.

Jessa glanced out the window again and saw Russ and Jay striding towards the chapel, both carrying travel-coffee mugs.

"Yikes! I'm late!" Jessa stuffed both letters in her pocket and skittered down the stairs, jogging to catch up with the guys. She got to the chapel just behind them, out of breath. She said good-morning to Jay and Russ, then smoothed her pony-tail and walked over to her microphone. One thing was for sure; she needed to ask Marsha for advice about these letters, and soon.

At lunch, Jessa seized the opportunity to talk to Marsha, nudging her discreetly the moment she finished her grilled-cheese sandwich.

"Hey." Jessa said quietly. "I need to talk to you!" Marsha grabbed a few celery sticks off her plate and followed Jessa out of the dining room and into the hall.

"Is this about Tiff?" Marsha asked quietly, her eyes wide.

"No, why?" Jessa asked.

"She missed the morning at the barn." Marsha said. "I guess she told Hank she had some family commitment. Hank's not too happy, though, because she was away yesterday afternoon, too, and we're already short. Apparently she'll be back this afternoon, and Hank is going to have a chat with her about it."

"It's not about Tiff." Jessa said. "It's this." She pulled out the two letters and showed them to Marsha. "Quick, read them. We only have a few minutes until we need to get to the barn."

Marsha read fast, then looked up at Jessa, perplexed. "So now two guys are writing you love letters? Would it kill them to sign their names?"

"I know!" Jessa said. "But that's not all. Yesterday Wade and I finally had a talk. He said I was his first choice all along, but he thought I didn't like him. He wants me to give us a chance."

"Oooh!" Marsha's face lit up. "Are you going to?"

"I don't know!" Jessa cried. "Do you think one of these is from him?"

"Only one way to find out." Marsha winked. "Meet the mystery man at the fireplace after chapel tonight."

"I suppose." Jessa groaned. "Can you hang around after chapel in case it's some weird creep from maintenance or something?"

"Is that code for Patrick?" Marsha snorted. "He could never have written this."

"I don't know." Jessa said darkly. "I have no idea what he's capable of. For all I know this is his idea of a prank, then I'll come off looking like some love-sick loser."

"You'll be fine." Marsha winked. "I mean, Jay and Russ will be there, too, right? Tidying up the stage and stuff? I'm sure they'll look out for you."

"True." Jessa gestured at the door. "You're off the hook, I guess. Come on, we've gotta go."

The rest of the wranglers had already left the dining hall, so Jessa and Marsha walked fast to get to the barn. That is; Marsha walked fast, and Jessa jogged to keep up with her long-legged friend. When they arrived, Wade, Nate, and Patrick were all hanging around near the watering trough.

Jessa headed for Fairlight, seeing that she was saddled and ready in her stall.

"Wait." Nate warned. "You may not want to go in the barn."

"Why?" Jessa asked.

"Tiff's back. Hank is talking to her in the office." He said ominously, popping his neon baseball cap on and off. "And it doesn't sound too pretty in there."

"But our one o clock trail ride starts in five minutes." Marsha reasoned. "I need to get my cowboy hat."

"I'm telling ya." Nate said. "I'd give them some space."

Just then Jessa heard a loud bellow coming from the barn. It sounded like Tiff's voice. Next thing she knew, the barn door had crashed open and Tiff charged out like a bull, stopping on the porch. Hank was right behind her, looking thunderous. Jessa had never seen his face so red.

"Don't you walk away from me, young lady." Hank said firmly.

"Well, if I'm fired, then you're not my boss anymore, right?" Tiff screeched. "So I don't have to listen to you! I can't believe what you're accusing me of, Hank!"

"So tell me the truth then. Where were you this morning? And yesterday afternoon?" Hank stood planted with his hands on his hips. Barb floated out behind him.

"I had stuff to do! I told you that!" Tiff yelled.

"You've been lying to me, Tiff, and sneaking around past curfew, too. Oh don't deny it; Ms. Sheila saw you coming in at three o clock in the morning the other night!" Hank shouted.

"I'm not a liar!" Tiff screamed.

"This isn't the first time you've shirked your work, and been caught out after hours, Tiff." Hank said. "You promised me it wouldn't happen again. Now it has. You've broken my trust, again, and that's it. You need to pack your things and go home."

"But Hank!" Tiff's voice turned into a whine. Jessa felt paralysed; she couldn't look away. "I'm sorry, Hank! What about forgiveness?"

"I do forgive you, Tiff." Hank said, more calmly. "That doesn't mean there aren't consequences for your actions. How many other people have you caught up in this web of lies?"

"I'm telling you I didn't lie!" Tiff said, choking back a sob. "I really did have a dentist appointment yesterday. I just...also went out with my boyfriend afterwards."

"You twisted the truth. Manipulated the facts. Just like this morning; when I'm sure you were out with said boyfriend again, instead of where you belonged."

"He called me and said he needed to see me urgently!" Tiff cried, tears running down her face. "And then the jerk dumped me in the parking lot. I'm so sorry Hank! Please don't send me away. There's only a few days left of camp!"

"I can't trust you, Tiff." Hank said firmly. "I wish it didn't have to be this way. I truly do. But I've given you more than one second chance down here, and you continue to have this deceitful, sly attitude. Now you've used up your chances and you need to leave."

"Hank, please!" Tiff wailed.

"Pack your things." Hank said shortly. "I'll call your parents to pick you up before dinner-time." He turned and stalked back into the barn, with Barb following after him silently.

"Nooooo!" Tiff shrieked and threw herself down on the porch floor, hugging a beam, her whole body wracking with sobs.

Jessa and Marsha looked at each other uneasily. As much as Tiff had driven Jessa crazy; she hadn't wanted her to get fired. And she seemed so broken now. Worse, campers would be arriving any minute and see Tiff in this state.

Wade was one of Tiff's oldest childhood friends, and now he walked over to Tiff and laid a gentle hand on her shoulder. Jessa heard Tiff blubber, "Oh, Wade, what have I done?" As he helped her to her feet.

"Jessa?" Wade called. "Can you ask Hank if I can take twenty minutes to help Tiff to the lodge? I was only scheduled for project-horse training right now anyway."

"Sure." Jessa breathed and went to knock on the office door. She creaked it open, seeing Hank sitting on the counter, his head in his hands, and Barb standing close to him.

"Sorry to interrupt, Hank." Jessa said meekly.

"Jessa, come in. It's okay. I'm sorry you had to see that. I probably could have handled it more calmly. I apologize." Hank said.

"No problem." Jessa said. "Wade asked if he can walk Tiff back up to the lodge."

"Sure." Hank nodded. "Or, better yet, I'll drive her up myself in the barn truck. I don't want to end things on that note."

Barb nodded her approval and passed him the keys. Hank stepped out of the office, leaving Jessa with Barb.

"Hey, Barb." Jessa said. "It's not always this dramatic around here, honestly." She chuckled a little. She thought

Barb had a hint of a smile in her lined face. Then, Barb spoke in her usual poetic way. Jessa had come to expect this quirk, and found it intriguing.

So many choices that we face
Roads and trails; which one to take?
Never lose hope that the Lord knows best
Which way will bring you peace and rest
Hold on to hope; God's perfect peace
Will come to you, his ways complete
Give him your heart, your dreams, your fire
He will reward a true heart's desire.

"Thanks, Barb." Jessa smiled politely. As usual she didn't understand what Barb was getting at, but she was learning to appreciate her unusual personality. "You really are a poet. Or a poetess, I suppose." To that Barb gave one long, solemn nod, and Jessa left the office.

Just before dinner that evening, Jessa and Marsha stopped at their lodge room. Tiff stood over her bed, stuffing clothes into a bag. She had already rolled up her sleeping bag and placed her pillow beside it. Her usually immaculate black braids looked messy and dishevelled. She was no longer crying, but her eyes were red.

"Jessa. Marsha." Tiff's voice cracked as she opened her arms to both of them. For a long moment she hugged them tightly, sobbing onto Marsha's neck. Her solid fist gripped Jessa's arm so tightly that she thought it might leave a mark, but Jessa didn't shake her off.

Finally, Tiff pulled back and looked at them. "My parents will be here in a few minutes." Tiff said, her voice gravelly. "I need to say goodbye. And I need to apologize." Tiff continued. "Especially to you, Jessa. I am obviously a total psycho when it comes to guys, hey?" She laughed a little, sniffling. "First I rip your head off about Wade, then I almost give in to Brady's black-mail, and now I've wrecked our friendship by going out with Clark."

"Oh, Tiff." Marsha said, rubbing Tiff's back.

"I'm a mess." Tiff proclaimed. "Why do I always do this? Why do I need my validation from guys? I mean, am I so insecure that I need a steady boyfriend to feel good about myself?" Tiff sat down on the edge of the bunk and twisted her braids in her hands. "I've ruined everything, and now I'm fired."

"Are you mad at Hank?" Marsha asked. Tiff shook her head.

"We had a good talk in the truck when he drove me back here. I don't blame him. I know he didn't want to do it but he felt he had no choice." Marsha nodded empathetically. Jessa stood a few feet away, feeling numb.

"I am the worst friend in the world." Tiff declared ruefully. "Please forgive me Jessa. I shouldn't have lied to you; probably shouldn't have dated your brother in the first place. You did ask me not to. I guess I took it as a challenge. I have serious issues."

"Stop saying that." Marsha chided.

"It's true!" Tiff exclaimed. "No one else around here leaves a wake of destruction and wrecked relationships in their path. Maybe I need counselling."

"You need to give your love-life to God." Jessa said suddenly, surprising herself. "You keep trying to control everything all the time. The tighter you hold on, the worse it gets." She started pacing, picking up steam.

"You may not like what I have to say, Tiff." Jessa said with authority. "But I am telling you this because I care about you."

"Okay?" Tiff said weakly.

"You try to control everything. I mean, I do that too; we probably all do to some degree; but you do it way too much. Like when you trained Polka-dot. You were too hard and demanding on him. He couldn't meet your expectations and he flipped out. That's why no one else can manage him now. He bucks and runs like a mustang.

He even bucked off Wade this morning." Tiff opened her mouth to retort, but Jessa kept going.

"And when you like a guy, you push so hard to get all his attention, and you end up driving him away. And drive all your friends away." Jessa slowed down. "You keep trying to run the show. You need to give your heart to God, and let him be the Lord of your life. He knows which guy you will end up with." Jessa stopped, seeing Tiff had tears in her eyes again.

"I'm already a Christian, Jessa." Tiff whimpered, somewhat defiantly. "I should know this already."

"Well maybe you needed a reminder. I mean, I needed the exact same reminder earlier this week; so I'm no wiser than you." Jessa admitted, sitting down beside Tiff. "We need to let go. We need to trust the Lord, knowing that there is a time for everything, and he has good plans for us."

"You know, I haven't even thought of giving my love-life to God." Tiff admitted. "What kind of horrible Christian am I?"

"You're not horrible." Jessa said. "You're simply not perfect. None of us are. That's why we need God in our lives. He'll show us what we need to do, so we don't have to try to do it all ourselves." Jessa pulled the two crumped letters from her pocket and opened the first one, searching for the verse and then reading aloud: 'Trust in the Lord with all of your heart, and lean not on your own understanding. In all your ways acknowledge him, and he will direct your paths. Proverbs 3:5."

"Jessa, are you going to become a pastor or something?" Marsha teased. "Preach it, girl!"

Jessa cracked a smile. "I am on a roll, aren't I?"

"I have to go." Tiff said, standing up. "My parents said they'd be here by now. I should get to the parking lot."

"Okay." Jessa said. "Just remember what I said, and try it."

"I'll try." Tiff, said giving her one last hug. "And Jessa, will you forgive me?"

"I will." Jessa said. "And we can still be friends. Let's keep in touch. Email me."

"Thanks, Jessa." Tiff picked up her bag. "I won't forget you guys. Ever."

CHAPTER 11
CROSSROADS AT THE CHAPEL

An hour later, Jessa stood next to Jay at the front of the chapel and checked her microphone. It just needed to be switched on. Kenny and his friends were already seated in the front row, and more campers were pouring in. The wranglers sat together in the back, and Jessa thought she heard Patrick say loudly, “There she is! My future girlfriend! She’s gonna go to the banquet with me!” She saw him pointing her way brazenly.

Rolling her eyes, Jessa glanced sideways at Jay. He looked amused.

“One of your loyal fans, I presume?” Jay teased. He wore his dreadlocks long and loose down his back today, and had a big hooded sweater on.

“Don’t ask.” Jessa groaned. “He’s one of many who keep trying to secure me as a date to the staff banquet.”

“Really?” Jay looked back at Patrick, who had turned his back her and hoisted one leg up onto the bench to tie his shoe. Patrick’s pants were far too low-cut, revealing an expansive white back-side. “Did you accept?” Jay’s eyes twinkled.

"No!" Jessa exclaimed, shuddering. "I don't see why everyone wants to pair off and get a date, anyway. It just makes things awkward. Isn't it better to just all go as friends?"

"You may have a point there." Jay said thoughtfully, picking up his guitar. "So the guys are all beating down your door to take you out, huh?"

"Yeah. It sucks." Jessa said gloomily, a hint of a smile still on her lips. The noise level in the chapel was starting to rise, as the campers got antsy waiting for worship to start.

"Maybe it's cause you don't have dreadlocks." Jay suggested slyly. "If you turned your hair into dreads, you'd turn all these potential suitors off, apparently. Less drama. Just a suggestion."

"Hey!" Jessa laughed. "I didn't mean-"

"No, no, you're probably right." Jay grinned. "If I cut off the dreads my love life may turn around. I'll take your word for it." Jessa gave him an apologetic look, then glanced back at Patrick.

"I just wish these guys would all stop bugging me about escorting them to the banquet. It's getting pretty irritating, but I don't have a good excuse to say no."

"Tell you what." Jay said, leaning closer to her. His eyes were green; like hers. "How about you and I go to the banquet together, as friends? That way you can tell those other young bucks that you're already going with someone. Cuts out the awkward drama." His eyes twinkled.

"Jay, are you asking me out?" Jessa teased, batting her eyes dramatically.

"Nah, you would have to ask *me*." Jay said. "I'd be doing you a favour, of course; helping you shake off those hounds." Jessa laughed with him.

"Fine. Jay, will you go to the banquet with me, as friends?" Jessa played along.

"I guess I could." Jay said thoughtfully. "Especially since there's no danger of you falling in love with me. Not as long as I have these dreads, right?"

"Oh brother." Jessa rolled her eyes again, and the lights dimmed. She stepped forward and switched her microphone on as lyrics appeared on the big screen.

"Helllooo campers!" Jay yelled into his microphone. "How is everybody doing tonight?" The campers went wild, screaming and clapping. The noise was tremendous. The drummer counted in the first song, and the campers all jumped around doing the actions.

Oooo-Oohh, God loves me.
Oooo-Oohh, God loves you.
Oooo-Oohh God loves everybody
In the whole wide world, Oh yeah!
Stomp your feet, clap your hands,
Jump around, everybody dance!
Oooo-Oohh, God loves me.
Oooo-Oohh, God loves you.
Oooo-Oohh God loves everybody!

As they sang four more fast-paced worship songs, Jessa started to feel nervous. After the singing Russ would lead the scripture-reading; then Bill would speak for twenty minutes or so. Then, she was supposed to meet her mystery admirer at the fire-place.

Jessa lost track of the words she was supposed to be singing for a minute, and looked down at the music stand to find her place. Her mind was starting to wander, as she worried about how the conversation would go, and who it even was she was meeting. She hadn't had a chance to check the letters to see if the guy meeting her tonight was the same one who had been writing all week.

Trust me.

Jessa didn't hear audible words, but she sensed God was reminding her to let go of the control and trust him. Taking a deep breath and starting to sing again, Jessa said in her heart, *I will trust you with my love-life, Lord. I need you, here!*

The song ended and Jessa sat down between Jay and

Kenny. The bench was as full as it could be; Jessa was sitting close to Jay; her leg pressing against his. Jessa again could smell the sharp, fresh scent of his aftershave.

Russ got up and had a camper read a bible verse, but Jessa couldn't concentrate. She felt oddly light, and giddy. Perhaps it was a high from singing on stage. An adrenalin rush. Or maybe it was the excitement of knowing she would soon find out who was writing her the mystery-letters.

Bill got up to speak, and Jessa was having a hard time paying attention to anything he said. She was aware of the warmth of Jay's arm, right beside hers. There was no space on her other side to move away; but then, she didn't want to get away. She wanted to stay right where she was.

Looking to the floor, Jessa saw that her cowboy boots were scuffed and battered. Jay's foot was right next to hers, stretched out casually. He wore red-and-blue high tops with yellow laces. His shoes clashed atrociously with cheetah-print board shorts.

Jessa forced herself to look up at Bill and try to pay attention. All she could hear were words; and they didn't make any sense. She couldn't process what he was saying. She felt her fingers and toes tingling, like she was holding onto a live-wire; but she didn't know why. Her left leg started bouncing up and down.

"Hey." Jay whispered, elbowing her gently. "You're jiggling the whole bench."

"Sorry." Jessa murmured and looked at him. He was right beside her, smiling mischievously. She locked eyes with him, feeling on fire. It was like looking into a bright light. A green light.

"And THAT," Bill stepped right in front of them, and they both jumped and broke the connection, "Is exactly why God sent his son Jesus to die for us. You see..." Jessa glazed over again as Bill continued.

Finally Bill wrapped up his lesson, and said a long prayer. Jessa closed her eyes but didn't listen. *Lord, what is going on in my heart?* She wondered frantically.

Jessa stayed where she was on the front row as the campers were dismissed. Everyone was jumping up and rushing for the door; clamouring to get to the lodge for evening snack.

"See ya, Jess!" Kenny said as he bounded away.

"Night, Kenny!" Jessa called.

"You got them, Erik?" Jay called out to his co-counsellor. "I have some stuff to finish up here."

"No prob." Erik waved and followed the campers out. Jay strode back to the front and unplugged his guitar. Russ trotted up, too, and started loading his bass into its case.

Jessa stood up and stretched, then slowly walked to the fireplace. It had been lit before chapel and crackled invitingly. She sat down on the stone hearth, looking into the flames.

"Jessa?" A male voice said behind her. Jessa turned, and her jaw dropped in disbelief.

"Nate?" Jessa said, shocked. "You're here?"

"Yeah." Nate said, holding out his arms with a smile. "It's me."

"I, I have to admit I'm surprised." Jessa said awkwardly. This hadn't been what she expected.

"I thought about our conversation." Nate said. "I realized you were right." He took off his baseball cap and twirled it around his fist.

"Our conversation?" Jessa frowned, thinking back. "What do you mean?"

Just then Patrick bounded over.

"There you are." Patrick bellowed, hiking up his pants. "You can't avoid me forever, pretty lady. Now, have you given anymore thought to what we talked about?"

"What?" Jessa blanched, just as Wade walked over, his cowboy hat in hand.

"Hey Jessa." Wade smiled warmly, then looked confusedly at Nate and Patrick. "Oh, sorry. I didn't mean to interrupt. I was just hoping we would have a chance to talk."

"But I need to talk to her, first." Nate said firmly.

"Guys, butt out." Patrick said loudly. "It's clear I'm the one who-"

"Hey, guys, what's goin' on?" Jay wandered over, a microphone cord looped over his arm. Russ followed, holding an armful of papers.

"I- I don't know who-" Jessa trailed off, bewildered. Wade, Patrick, Nate, Russ, and Jay were all looking back at her expectantly.

"Um, did any of you have something specific to talk to me about?" She squeaked at last.

"Yeah, I do-" Nate started but Patrick interrupted.

"Back off, man, she still hasn't given me an answer about the banquet!"

"Jessa, I thought we could talk more about-" Wade started.

"It's important!" Nate said hotly, cutting Wade off. "Jessa, can we go somewhere private?"

"Look, fellas." Jay said good-naturedly. "You're all freaking Jessa out. Please, one at a time." Jessa gave him a grateful look.

"Okay, me first." Patrick said forcefully. "Jessa, honey, I want to take you to the banquet. I'll treat ya real nice."

"No thanks, Patrick." She said.

"You don't mean that." Patrick said tauntingly. "You're just playing hard-to-get. I know it's a ploy of all women-folk. Come on, now." He stepped forward and grasped Jessa's arm.

"Patrick, let go!" Jessa tried to wrench her arm free. Wade and Nate both lunged forward and pulled Patrick off her. Wade looked thunderous. Jay sprang forward to help, too, but she was already free by the time he reached her. Patrick wriggled out of Wade's grip, irritated.

"Geez. Can't you guys take a joke? It's all in fun."

Patrick said and stalked away, letting the chapel door slam behind him as he left.

"You okay, Jessa?" Nate asked, concerned. Jessa nodded, startled. "Okay. Well, look, clearly this isn't a good time. Can we talk later? It's about the binder." He hinted.

"Oh!" Jessa said, profoundly relieved. "That's all you wanted to talk to me about? The binder?"

"Well, yeah." Nate said, confused. "What did you think I wanted to talk about?"

"Never mind. Yeah, I'll catch you later." She waved as Nate left. Jay continued clearing up the stage as Wade stepped closer.

"So." Wade smiled, the glow from the firelight dancing across his face. "You're here."

"So are you." Jessa shrugged nervously. Out of the corner of her eye she saw Jay chatting with Russ near the guitars. "So, you wanted to....?"

"Talk." Wade filled in for her. "Yes, it's time. Jessa, I hope you believe me when I say I really like you. We've had too many missed chances and miscommunications this summer. But none of that matters now." Jessa was trying to pay attention but she couldn't help notice Jay as he turned to move a music stand, the fire-light illuminated his features. He was laughing at something Russ had said. Jessa had never before appreciated his strong jaw, and muscular arms.

"Jessa, I like you." Wade said, moving closer and reaching out to hold her by the elbows. She forced herself to look up at him. His expression was ardent and sincere. She should be jubilant. She should be ecstatic. She should feel electricity and tingles up and down her arms. Shouldn't she? So why couldn't she concentrate on a word Wade was saying?

"I want you to be my girlfriend. I'm asking you to be. Be with me, and let's see where we can go as a couple." Wade said, willing her to say yes.

Jessa noticed Jay had fallen quiet and was rifling through sheets of lyrics on a music-stand. She hoped Jay hadn't heard Wade's question; but she was sure he had.

"Just say yes." Wade whispered. "Say yes to us, Jessa."

"I-" Jessa swallowed, fighting the urge to step back. This was what she had dreamed about all summer. Surely Marsha was right; she should at least give it a chance. So why did it feel so wrong to say yes?

"I-" She tried again but her throat stuck.

"Jessa?" Wade frowned, then looked over at Jay. "What are you looking at over there?"

"Nothing!" Jessa said quickly, pasting on a smile and tearing her gaze away from Jay.

"So, what do you think?" Wade said. "Are you ready to give us a chance?" He drew her closer to him.

"Um," Jessa fidgeted. She wished Wade would let go of her arms. He felt entirely too close and she needed room to breathe; to think. "It's just; I want to say yes, but doesn't something feel a bit off?" She said quietly. Wade frowned and let go of her arms, shifting backwards a step.

"Is this about Virginia, again?" Wade asked.

"No, no, it's not about Virginia." Jessa said. "It's about me."

"But then why did you agree to meet me here? I assume you got my letter?"

"Yes, I got all of your letters." Jessa said quickly. "And they were wonderful. They encouraged me so much this week. I really appreciated them."

"Wait a minute." Wade said. "What do you mean letters; plural? I only sent you one letter."

"You did?" Jessa said, cocking her head. "Then, who sent the other letters?"

"Me." Jessa jumped at the sound of Jay's voice. He stood several feet away, his arms full of papers, but he was looking right at her. "Sorry, I couldn't help but overhear." He dropped the papers and walked a step closer. Wade was staring at Jay; a look of shock on his face.

"You have been sending Jessa letters?" Wade said slowly. "Why?" Jay sighed, a calm strength exuding from him. The firelight flickered across his face, making him look like a bronze statue.

"Jessa, I know this may not be the time or the place." Jay said, looking straight at her. It was as though Wade wasn't even there, standing between them. "There's probably a million other, more epic ways I could do this. But time's running out; and I know if I don't tell you how I feel, I'll regret it forever."

Jessa was incapable of speech. She felt hypnotized; she couldn't tear her eyes off Jay. Her heart beat fast as Jay continued.

"Jessa, I never believed in love-at-first sight before. I thought it was romantic nonsense. But that was before I first saw you; that first day of camp in the parking lot. You were walking along the path in a pink t-shirt, and I was trying to get my guitars out of my van. I looked over and saw you, and instantly, I knew."

"Knew what?" Jessa whispered, her pulse thudding in her ears.

"I knew I had to win your heart." Jay smiled. "That's why I did whatever I could to get to know you. That's why I wrote you those letters. And every day this summer I've prayed for you; and just hoped God might turn your heart to me." As his honest words washed over her, Jessa couldn't help it; her face burst into a smile.

"Uh, hello?" Wade said indignantly, breaking her out of her revere. "If you don't mind, Jay, Jessa and I were kind of in the middle of a conversation, here."

"I'm sorry." Jay said, raising his hands. "I didn't mean to intrude. And Jessa, I want you to know there is no pressure on you. I'm not asking anything of you. I just had to be honest. I've been struggling all summer with whether or not to speak, and I never felt peace about it until now. I wanted to be a friend to you; and let you decide for yourself if you wanted anything more. Now you know; and you can do whatever you want with the information. If you end up with someone else; that's cool. I want you to know I'll always remember you, and hope you're happy, whatever you decide."

"Great." Wade said firmly. "Now can you let me finish our conversation?"

"Sure." Jay grinned impishly. "Sorry if I cramped your style, bro. See you guys later." He winked and strode to the door. Jessa fought the urge to run after him. She wasn't even sure what she would say; but her instinct was not to let him go.

Too late. He was gone.

"Now. Where were we?" Wade stepped closer again. This time, Jessa stepped back. She was feeling so many different things at one time; she was confused. All she knew is she couldn't do this. She couldn't stay here with Wade.

"Jessa?" Wade faltered.

"I'm sorry Wade." Jessa whispered. "I can't. I just can't."

"Why?" Wade said, a hurt look crossing his eyes.

"I'm so sorry, Wade." Jessa sidestepped him and hurried towards the door.

"Jessa!" He called after her. Jessa didn't look back. She blasted outside and took off running.

CHAPTER 12
TOO LITTLE, TOO LATE

Jessa burst into the sanctuary of her lodge room and slammed the door behind her. Marsha must still be down at snack; but she would likely be up soon and Jessa needed to hash this out. The overhead light was too bright. Jessa snapped on the lamp instead and switched the overhead lights out. Kicking off her boots, she paced the room like an anxious cat.

It was now quite dark outside; Jessa looked out the window and could barely see the path below. Looking up, she could still make out the silhouettes of the tree tops all around the lodge. She jerked the dingy curtains shut, not wanting to chance anyone seeing her.

Nibbling her nails, Jessa strode the small room in circles, until finally the door opened. Jessa pounced at Marsha and dragged her the rest of the way into the room, locking the door behind her.

"Marsha, we need to talk!" Jessa blurted out.

"What's wrong?" Marsha said, concerned.

"Everything's a mess. I hardly know where to start." Jessa said.

"Sit down." Marsha pointed to her bed. "Try starting at the beginning. Oh, and by the way, you missed cinnamon buns."

"Whatever. I'm not hungry." Jessa shrugged. "Marsha, Wade finally asked me out; and I freaked out and ran away!"

"No!" Marsha gasped. "Jessa how could you do that to the poor guy? Have you just been playing him all along?"

"Marsha, of course not!" Jessa cried. "I've been so confused and muddled. I thought I really still liked him. But the closer he got to me the more I wanted to run away."

"You're just new at this!" Marsha insisted. "Of course you're a little nervous; you've never dated before!"

"It's not that." Jessa shook her head. "It felt wrong. Like, the closer he got to me, the less attracted to him I felt. Like; the idea of kissing him repulsed me."

"Oh." Marsha said, disappointed. "Well, I admit that isn't a good sign."

"Right?" Jessa jumped up, pacing again. "It's like I had a crush on the idea of a crush. The idea of dating Wade. But when it was actually an option, I realized I don't even like Wade! Not that way."

"Poor chump." Marsha said. "Now I feel bad for encouraging him to try."

"I know." Jessa said miserably. "I don't know how I can face him again. But Marsha, there's more."

"What?" Marsha crossed her long legs.

"It's, it's about Jay." Jessa said awkwardly. "Lately, I've been feeling...well…"

"You like Jay?" Marsha gaped. Jessa flopped back down on the bed, burying her face in the pillow and talking muffled gibberish. "Okay, I can't understand you with a mouthful of pillow." Marsha gently rolled her over so she was face-up. "Try again."

Jessa swallowed. "Jay is the one who was writing me

the encouragement letters. He said he knew as soon as he first met me that he had to win me over. I'm just so shocked."

"That's a pretty gutsy thing to say, out of the blue." Marsha commented. Jessa nodded.

"It is, isn't it? It's totally forward and crazy. The thing is, lately I think I've started having feelings for him, too. I was just so distracted by Wade that I didn't even notice my heart was turning to Jay." Jessa tried to organize her jumbled thoughts.

"So let me get this straight." Marsha said, holding up her fingers. "You thought you liked Wade; but you actually like Jay, and he likes you back? That's the facts in a nutshell."

"Right." Jessa fidgeted. "That's the long and short of it."

"So what did you say to Jay when he told you about his feelings?"

"Nothing. I was in shock." Jessa said. "Wade was right there."

"You need to tell him." Marsha said. "Jay. You need to tell Jay how you feel!"

"But Marsha!" Jessa hollered, startling even herself. "It's so wild, isn't it? It's so unexpected. It's so scary. And exciting. Is it supposed to be this way?"

"Love is not always neat and tidy." Marsha said wisely. "But Jay is a good guy, right? He's a strong Christian, loves the Lord, and has been waiting patiently for you to notice him all summer, right?"

"Yeah." Jessa nodded, her heart warm.

"Do you feel peace about moving forward with Jay, and seeing where God takes you together?" Marsha continued.

"I do." Jessa said, realizing it was true.

"Then you have nothing to fear." Marsha dictated. "The way forward is clear. Tell him the truth." Jessa suddenly remembered Nate saying earlier in the summer 'the truth will set you free.' Right after that, she recalled the verse Jay had written her in one of his letters; about the Lord making her paths straight.

She knew now why it had felt so wrong to say yes to Wade. That path was the wrong direction for her. She needed to step out in faith on this new path; the one God had made clear for her. And she needed to do it soon.

Jessa slept fitfully that night. Several times she prayed that God would show her what to say to Jay; and how and where and when. She was dreadfully excited. She couldn't believe she had spent so much time and energy thinking about Wade; he was a friend and nothing more, and never would be more. Her heart belonged to Jay.

Finally at six, Jessa got out of bed and showered. She wanted to look her best, so she took extra time with her hair and make-up, and slipped into a fresh pair of jeans. Her plan was to go down early to the dining hall for a cup of hot chocolate. Several times throughout the summer, she had done just that, and often run into Jay and Russ having coffee in their pyjama-pants.

Jessa breezed down the stairs, her heart starting to pound. She was nervous; but it was a good-nervous. Excited. She would tell Jay she wanted to speak to him privately, and take him on a nice walk. Maybe they could walk to the creek again.

Jessa peeked her head into the kitchen. Tony and Cory-Lynn were mixing up muffins for breakfast and pouring the batter out into tins.

"Morning, Jessa!" Tony said. "You're sure up early."

"Yeah. Morning." Jessa craned her head, scanning the dining room. Nate's parents sat together at a table, drinking coffee and looking through their white binder, but Jay was nowhere in view.

"Can you believe it's Friday?" Cory-Lynn said

cheerily. "Last day of camp!"

"We've still got our staff banquet tomorrow, remember." Tony said. "I've got quite the feast planned. Roast beef, mashed potatoes…" He continued on as Jessa tried to nod along while simultaneously watched the door. Jay could come in all sleepy-eyed any minute; his hands stuffed into the pockets of his hooded sweater.

"It's crazy about Jay, huh?" Cory-Lynn said.

"What?" Jessa said, distractedly. "Oh, yeah. Totally crazy."

"It's so sad he had to leave like that." Cory-Lynn continued, catching a drip of batter with her finger just before it globbed on the counter. It took a moment for Jessa to register what Cory-Lynn was saying.

"Wait a minute, what?" Jessa asked, puzzled. "He had to leave?"

"Yeah." Cory-Lynn nodded. "Ms. Sheila told him right at the end of snack last night. I guess you weren't there. He had some family emergency and had to leave pretty quickly. He may not even be back at all." Jessa felt cold.

"I can't believe this." She murmured. "What happened?"

"We don't know for sure." Cory-Lynn said. "Russ said Jay's mom or sister got in a car accident or something, but he didn't get any details. He just had to go right away."

"Wow." Jessa said, leaning against the counter for support. "And he may not come back?"

"I don't think so." Cory-Lynn said sadly. "It's too bad; especially for his campers. At least they still have Erik."

"Uh-huh." Jessa said mechanically, backing towards the door. "Okay, well, see you later."

"There's still worship practice today!" Cory-Lynn called after her. "Russ is stepping in to the lead role." Jessa waved her acknowledgement and left the kitchen.

Worship practice was totally different without Jay. Russ led the practice just fine, but for Jessa, the zest had gone out of it. She sang along robotically. The band had a prayer time for Jay and his family, and Jessa was antsy to leave the moment Russ said 'Amen'.

"Hold on a sec, Jessa." Russ called when she was halfway to the door. She turned reluctantly as he jogged down the aisle towards her, his tear-away pants flapping against his bony legs.

"Here." Russ held out a string friendship-bracelet. "Jay had to leave in a hurry. He took this off his wrist and asked me to give it to you." Jessa took it and looked at it closely. The threads were blue and pink, woven together in an intricate braid.

"Thanks." Jessa said, running her thumb over it. "Did he make it?"

"No idea." Russ shrugged. "He said he'd never forget you; and he hopes when you look at the bracelet you'll remember him."

"Okay." Jessa whispered. "Can you help me put it on?" Russ tied in around her wrist then jogged back to the front of the chapel. Jessa slipped out and strode to the barn, her heart heavy.

Jessa felt more and more regret that she hadn't realized her feelings for Jay sooner. She thought back to some of the times they'd spent together; having hot chocolate together in the early-morning at the dining hall, worship practice, walking to the creek, singing together. Now she knew Jay had had feelings for her the whole time. *How could I have been so blind?* Jessa thought wretchedly as she crossed the meadow to the barn.

Jessa pushed open the barn gate and chanced to look over at the arena. What she saw made her stop short.

Patrick was waddling around the arena, leading Fairlight on a long lead-rope.

Jessa didn't think. She scrambled over the arena fence and ran at them, her eyes wild and her teeth bared.

"Get your hands off her!" Jessa screamed as she approached. Patrick took a step back, startled, and Fairlight jumped as well. Jessa grabbed the rope and ripped it out of Patrick's grubby hand. "Don't you touch her, Patrick!"

"Whoa, whoa!" Patrick put up his hands, stepping back again. "Simmer down, there, cowgirl! You gotta take a chill pill!"

"I told you I didn't want you riding her! You'll ruin her! You'll ruin everything!" Jessa bellowed, shaking a fist at Patrick. In the heat of the moment she knew she was over-reacting, but she didn't care. Her raw emotions needed an outlet and Patrick was ripe for the plucking.

"Calm down, Jessa!" Patrick yelled back. "Is this your PMS hormones again?"

Jessa opened her mouth to yell at Patrick some more, but stopped at the sight of Barb. She hadn't noticed her at the far end of the arena. Barb was standing with Polka-dot, who was completely untethered without even a halter on. He was nuzzling Barb's palm.

Barb looked back at Jessa evenly, then turned away and whispered something to Polka-dot. Then, she swung herself up onto his bare back with the grace of a dancer.

To Jessa's surprise, Polka-dot did not run or buck, but stood still, his ears pricked towards Barb. Barb said something to him, and he stepped out in a calm walk. Barb sat easily on his back, holding on to his brown and white mane with one hand.

"Are you done yelling at me, then?" Patrick said sarcastically. "Only Hank asked me to walk Fairlight for you. She had a slight limp this morning so Hank wanted her led around to warm up her joints."

"Oh." Jessa said, shamefaced. "So you weren't going to ride her?"

"No." Patrick said scornfully. "I wouldn't want to risk

getting in the way of your woman-rage."

"Patrick..." Jessa growled.

"Okay, okay!" Patrick exclaimed. "So if you're done biting my head off I have more work to do." Patrick turned on his thick heel and started towards the barn.

"Patrick." Jessa called after him grudgingly, and he half-turned. "I'm sorry for yelling at you. You didn't deserve that. I'm having a bad day and I took it out on you. I'm sorry, okay?" Patrick shrugged and kept walking.

Jessa sighed and leaned against Fairlight's neck, breathing in her warm scent. Tears sprang to her eyes as she realized she only had another twenty-four hours with Fairlight. She stifled a sob in the filly's black mane, wrapping her arms around her golden neck.

After a while, something warm nudged her on her shoulder. Jessa turned and saw that Barb had ridden Polka-dot up behind her. Barb's tanned face was as much an enigma as ever, but her eyes looked sorrowful.

Jessa didn't bother to hide her tears. She saw how Barb sat so peacefully on Polka-dot, earning his obedience with the lightest touch, bareback and without a bridle or halter.

"Teach me." Jessa mumbled, looking up at Barb's face. "Teach me to ride like that."

Barb looked at her for a long moment, studying her. Then, she bowed her head in agreement.

CHAPTER 13
FIND ANOTHER WAY

Much later that day, Jessa hobbled into the empty staff lounge. She had spent the better part of the day riding with Barb. They had skipped lunch; Jessa had no appetite anyway, and Barb had taught Jessa to ride without any saddle or bridle.

Jessa had giggled excitedly as Barb opened the arena gate and gestured for her to follow. Jessa rode Fairlight bareback with only a halter, and Barb rode Polka-dot with no rope of any kind. She had used leg pressure to tell Polka-dot what to do. They had ridden down to the creek and through the west pasture, where the August sun had blazed brightly on them as they trotted through grassy meadows.

Barb hadn't said much, predictably, but she hadn't needed to. When Jessa asked her how to get Fairlight responding, Barb would answer simply; *'Fairlight will show you everything you need to know. Trust her.'*

Twice Jessa had fallen off; once when they were trotting and Fairlight swerved unexpectedly to the right, and once when she scrambled up an embankment. But

Barb wasn't concerned, and Jessa wasn't hurt. She had heaved herself back up onto Fairlight's warm back and carried on.

As they had ridden back to the barn, Jessa knew that she would never forget that ride. It would become a golden, rosy memory to treasure, always. Now, as Jessa flopped onto the faded lounge couch, she dialled her parents' number. It rang three times before Clark answered.

"Well hey, kid. How's it going?"

"Hey Clark. I'm good. Can I talk to mom?"

"Sure. Just a sec." Her brother said.

"Is that my Jess-Jess?" Nancy's voice came through.

"Hi mom." Jessa said, sinking deeper into the couch. "How's it going?"

"Oh we are all good here, Jess. How about you and Kenny?"

"Fine." Jessa said. "Kenny is good; I saw him at breakfast. He seems to be having fun, but his counsellor had to leave early."

"Jay?" Nancy asked.

"Yeah."

"That's too bad." Nancy said. "He seemed stellar."

"He is." Jessa said, toying with the blue and pink bracelet on her wrist. "He's actually really cool, mom. He's kind, and funny, and loves God."

"And you like each other." Nancy added with a flourish.

"Mom!" Jessa squawked, sitting up. "How did you know?"

"I think I know my own daughter well enough." Nancy said proudly. "Hon, it's been pretty obvious. You've been talking about him all summer, on the weekends. Isn't he the one who lent you his guitar, and told you to hold out for a hero?"

"Yes."

"And it was all over both of your faces when we

dropped Kenny off on Monday." Nancy said. "The chemistry between you was sizzling."

"Oh, mom." Jessa said sheepishly. "You can read me like a book. The thing is I don't think I even realized until this week, and now it's too late to do anything. I haven't even told him. And he had to leave early; and I may never see him again."

"Jessa." Her mom sighed lovingly. "You always were the last one to figure these things out, weren't you? I know you were distracted by that cowboy for a while."

"Wade's just not right for me, though." Jessa said. "I realized that once and for all last night. That was just a crush. There was no depth. But with Jay..."

"It could be something real." Nancy finished for her. "Aw, my baby girl is growing up so fast."

"What should I do?" She implored her mom.

"Give it to God." Nancy said. "Remember? He's in control here."

"That's it?"

"And also, track him down and tell him. Ruth and Boaz-style." Nancy suggested.

"What?" Jessa frowned, confused.

"Remember Ruth, in the bible? She knew she wanted Boaz and she went right to him and told it like it was." Nancy said.

"Isn't that a little forward?" Jessa said. "Shouldn't I be playing hard to get?"

"Why?" Nancy demanded.

"Oh. Um, I don't know, I just thought that was how it's done." Jessa said lamely.

"Jessa, don't mess him around or play games. You wouldn't want him to do that to you, would you?" Nancy asked.

"No." Jessa admitted.

"Then be honest. Whatever will be will be." Nancy said. "Here, your dad wants to talk to you."

"Jess?" Eugene picked up the phone.

"Hi dad."

"Did you make an offer to Hank about that horse you wanted to buy?" Eugene asked.

"Yeah." Jessa said, her spirits falling again. "He said no. He said she's worth twice what I offered." Her dad was silent for a moment, considering.

"That's a shame." He said.

"Yes. I cried." Jessa said flatly. "But I've done all I can. He said no and that's the end of it."

"Jessa, do you really want this horse?" Her dad asked.

"Of course I do." She said. "You know that." A lump rose in her throat. "But it's no use. Hank said no."

"If you really want her, you should keep trying. There's a time for everything. That's in Ephesians, I believe. Jessa, there's a time to let go, and there's a time to try harder. If this is something you really want you shouldn't give up without a fight."

"But dad." Jessa said brokenly. "I can't afford her. Not even half."

"Is there any possible solution you can imagine to come up with the money? Think." Her dad urged her. Jessa considered briefly what her dad was hinting at.

"You mean, would you and mom consider loaning me the money?" Jessa asked slowly.

"There you go." Her dad sounded pleased. "All this time all you had to do was ask."

"Dad, do you really mean it? You will lend me the money?" Jessa cried.

"Of course we will, Hun." Her dad sounded surprised. "You know we support you with your riding one-hundred percent. Go ahead and make the counter-offer, and we can work-out a payment plan between ourselves."

"Okay." Jessa said, her heart filling with hope.

"Try, at least." Her dad advised. "Make sure he understands how much you want her. Then make the offer. And give us a call about when we should borrow a horse trailer and come pick her up."

Dinner that evening was a somewhat awkward affair; partially because Wade had a moody, forlorn look about him. Patrick seemed more obnoxious than usual, too. Jessa tried to be extra pleasant, feeling she owed both of them some slack over her erratic behaviour lately.

"Jessa!" Nate said when he arrived at the table, bearing a loaded tray of tacos. "Finally. You missed lunch, and I still need to tell you the big news."

"Is this about," Jessa lowered her voice and leaned closer, "The binder?"

"Yep." Nate nodded and slathered hot-sauce over his tacos. "And it's not really a secret after all, as everyone else already knows."

"So what is it? What's all the hooplah?" Jessa badgered.

"Okay, so you know how my parents have been all weird and secretive, and have this big binder with your name in it?" Nate said, shoving his dark hair out of his eyes. "Well, I took your advice and just asked my dad man-to-man what it was, yesterday before chapel. So he and my mom finally spilled the beans, and it's not a bad thing after all. I was sure they were getting divorced or deported or something."

"Deported?" Jessa said, confused. "Why, are they illegal immigrants?"

"Huh?" Nate said. "You lost me."

"Never mind, continue." Jessa urged.

"Okay, brace yourself." Nate grinned. "Are you braced?"

"Nate just say it already!" Jessa demanded.

"Our whole family is moving here, to Sun Valley!" He announced triumphantly.

"What! Wow!" Jessa squeaked. "That's amazing!"

"I know." Nate said, taking a big bite of taco. Hot sauce splattered over his chin but he kept talking. "I guess they've been talking about it for a while and going over details. They just didn't want to tell us kids until it was a sure thing."

"Are you all moving to camp permanently? To join the winter staff?" Jessa asked.

"No, we're renting some duplex in the town of Sun Valley. My dad is going to keep his principal position at his school in the city, though, and commute for a while. But you don't know the best part yet."

"What is it?"

"They've enrolled me in your school!" Nate said, wiping his chin with a napkin. "Sun Valley Christian, right? We'll be in the same class."

"That's great!" Jessa reached over and gave him a side hug, careful to avoid the taco-sauce dribbled down his t-shirt. "I'm so excited! You'll love it, it's a great school."

"That's why your name was in the binder." Nate explained. "My parents had been making pros and cons lists about different schools, and they thought it was a pro that we would be in the same class, since that way I'll already know someone there."

"Definitely. This is so fantastic!" Jessa said, picking up her own taco.

Just then Hank appeared in the doorway, and scanned the tables. When he spotted Jessa he started straight over and was talking before he reached her.

"Hey gang. Jessa, we need to talk. Barb explained that, well, she helped me see that"- Hank stopped and glanced around the table. "Let's go to the staff lounge, where we can talk privately." Hank said firmly.

"Okay." Jessa pushed back her chair. "I wanted to talk to you anyway."

"Good." Hank said, nabbing a cucumber slice off Nate's plate and dipping it in the taco Nate was about to bite in to. "After you, Jessa." He gestured for the door and popped the cucumber in his mouth.

CHAPTER 14
WHERE THERE'S A WILL, THERE'S A WAY

"You look stunning." Marsha said the following evening, stepping back to admire her handiwork. "Absolutely stunning. You're going to knock him to the floor."

"You think so?" Jessa admired herself in the lodge-room mirror. Marsha had just finished styling Jessa's hair for her, and now it hung it rich brown curls half-way down her back. The summer sun had highlighted it naturally, making it shine.

"Absolutely. Let me put a little more hair-spray in." Marsha leaned forward. "I'm glad you put the dress on, first." She nodded at the simple but flattering black sun-dress Jessa wore with sandals. "It's a really nice dress, by the way. I've never seen it before."

"My mom dropped it off this afternoon when she picked up Kenny." Jessa said. "She's a bit of a romantic. She said I might want to wear in to the banquet, just in case Jay makes it back in time."

"Right. Officially you were supposed to go together, right?" Marsha said, spraying some perfume on Jessa's neck.

"Whoa, easy!" Jessa laughed and stepped away as Marsha poised the perfume bottle for an extra squirt. "Yes, we were going to go together. But that's only if he gets back in time. Apparently he talked to Russ on the phone this morning and said he would try his best."

"It's so lucky that his mom's car accident wasn't serious." Marsha said. "Thank God."

"I know." Jessa said, remembering Russ's update at lunch. "She walked away, even though the car was totalled."

"Are you nervous?" Marsha asked, touching up her own make-up. "What are you going to say to Jay?"

"I don't know yet." Jessa said, examining the blue and pink friendship bracelet on her wrist. "The truth, I guess."

"Are you excited?" Marsha nudged.

"Yes." Jessa said simply, and looked at the clock. "It's time."

"Okay." Marsha beamed. "You look beautiful. The best I've ever seen you. Let's go."

The banquet was being held in the chapel; where all the pews had been replaced with round tables. The tables were covered in multi-colored sheets, which Ms. Sheila lovingly called 'table-cloths.' The tables were graced with flickering tea-light candles and tin-cans stuffed with ferns and wild-flowers. A local country band had been hired to play, and were already twanging out a song under a canopy of tiny white fairy lights.

"This is like a wedding reception!" Marsha gasped in delight as they stepped inside. Jessa barely saw any of it. She was scanning the tables, looking for Jay. She didn't see him.

"Good evening, my ladies!" Nate approached, his hair slicked back from a center-part, and an elaborate bow-tie clipped onto his t-shirt. "May I escort you to your table?"

"With pleasure." Marsha giggled and took his arm. Nate offered his other arm to Jessa but she was distracted by a tall, clean-cut man in a tuxedo. He was walking straight towards her.

There was something vaguely familiar about him. He had a strong, athletic build, and a confident gate. His short brown hair was artfully styled, making it look wind-blown. He was tanned, and smiling, revealing even white teeth. But the most striking of his features were his eyes; which were fixed on her with an intense expression of delight.

Jessa stared at him, dumbfounded as he approached. Marsha and Nate melted away. He stopped in front of her, a confident smile on his face. It wasn't until she saw the twinkle of his green eyes that she realized who it was.

"Jay?" She gulped. Jay chuckled, then bowed playfully.

"At your service, Jessa." He said gallantly, his eyes glowing. He noticed the blue and pink bracelet on her wrist and his smile deepened.

"You look so different." Jessa said, agog. "Your dreadlocks..."

"Got chopped off, as per your suggestion." He grinned. "My sister did it for me this morning. She was also the one to suggest the tux."

"Wow." Jessa said, staring at him. "Just, wow."

"Aw, knock it off, you're going to puff up my head." Jay grinned, looking proud of himself. "You look gorgeous, as usual."

"Thanks." Jessa said. "I just can't believe you actually cut off your dreads."

"Well, I had a tip-off that I might have a better chance coaxing you to go out with me if I got rid of them." Jay teased. "And now here we are."

"Yes, here we are." Jessa beamed back at him. She was quite honestly flabbergasted by how good he looked.

He barely looked like the same person.

"I'd be honoured to escort you to the banquet, if you like." Jay said, offering his arm. "We had agreed to go as friends, I recall?"

"I'd be delighted." Jessa said, taking his arm. Jay pulled her arm through his and grasped her hand.

"Good." Jay said, starting to walk to their table. "Though I can't pretend what I feel for you is strictly friend-zone."

Jessa looked evenly back in his green eyes and shyly answered, "Me neither."

Jay squeezed her hand again, and led her to sit with Marsha, Nate, Cory-Lynn, and Russ. He pulled out her chair for her, then settled in beside her, taking her hand. It felt right. Comfortable. Perfect.

"So, are you two like, together now?" Nate said loudly. Marsha dropped her napkin and looked at them expectantly. Jay turned to Jessa.

"Whatever Jessa says." He winked.

"I say yes." Jessa blushed, squeezing Jay's hand.

"Whoo-hoo!" Marsha jumped up from her chair and cheered. Nate looked confused but shrugged.

"Congrats, I guess." Nate said. "Hey, did you guys see Virginia is here?" He gestured to the next table, where Wade was sitting with Hank's stunning blond niece. "I guess Wade called her yesterday to invite her to the banquet."

"Hmm." Marsha said appraisingly. "They are certainly looking quite lovey-dovey."

"Happy for them." Jessa said simply, looking back at Jay. "Bless their hearts."

Dinner was served, and Tony had truly outdone himself with a fabulous meal. They had sparkling fruit punch served in plastic wine glasses, complete with floating berries. Then came cesar salad, followed by the main course of roast beef, mashed potatoes and gravy, vegetables, and dinner rolls. Dessert was a succulent raspberry-chocolate cheesecake.

The country band strummed along in the background, making the mood light and fun. After dinner some of the tables were cleared, and the dance-floor filled with people. Jay stood and offered her his hand.

"Would you like to dance?" He asked. Jessa rose and followed him onto the floor.

"I'm not much of a dancer." She apologized as he slipped his arms around her waist. He shrugged good-naturedly.

"Whatever. We'll pretend we are. It will be fun." He started swaying her to the music, then dipped her dramatically. Laughing, she twirled him in a circle and struck a pose, waving wild jazz-hands.

It was fun. It was so easy, and so right.

Settling back into his arms, Jessa rested her head on his shoulder and sighed. The lights were dimmed and the fairy lights twinkled overhead.

"So." Jay murmured into her hair. "You know I have to go back to college tomorrow."

"I know." Jessa said. "When will I see you again?"

"Hmm." Jay said, holding her closer, smiling like everything was right in his world. "It's only about three hours away. I can drive up and see you on the weekends, sometimes. If you want me to."

"I do." Jessa said, snuggling closer.

"Then I'll be there." Jay promised. "And we can email. And talk on the phone. You can always come out and see me, too."

"Okay." Jessa said dreamily. She melted into his arms as he rocked her back and forth to the honkey-tonk music. Across the room she could see Wade dancing with Virginia, looking bewitched. She chuckled, knowing Wade would be just fine. Marsha was dancing with Nate in a completely goofy, unromantic way. They seemed to be inventing new and corny dance-moves as a contest. For a moment Jessa wondered how Tiff was doing, and thought it was a shame she was missing this.

It was a beautiful send-off party for the staff. Jessa snuggled in closer to Jay's shoulder, feeling like a dream she hadn't even realized she had was coming true.

"Uh, hello? Is this on? Test, test." Russ squeaked into one of the microphones, causing the band to halt. "Hey, everyone. I have an announcement!" Russ smiled hugely. "The stunningly beautiful Cory-Lynn has just agreed to marry me!"

After a shocked silence, someone yelled, "Hurrah!", and then a raucous applause broke out over the crowd. Jessa laughed and clapped hard as the giggling, beet-red Cory-Lynn made her way up to the front. Russ wrapped his scrawny arms around her, victorious, and planted a big kiss on her lips.

"Wow." Jessa chuckled as Jay resumed dancing. "So soon."

"I guess when you know, you know." Jay winked at her and twirled her again.

"And you're claiming that with me, you knew from day one." Jessa teased him, poking him in the ribs.

"Ow!" Jay laughed, grabbing her hand tightly so she couldn't tickle him anymore. "Yes, I knew I had to somehow win you over."

"Then why didn't you say something a long time ago?" Jessa asked. "We could have had so much more time together. The whole summer."

"The time wasn't right." Jay said simply, stroking her back. "I felt like God was telling me to wait. There's a time for everything, you know."

"Yes, I've been hearing that." Jessa smiled. Just then Jessa felt someone tap her on the shoulder. Turning, she saw it was Hank.

"Hey, Jessa. Sorry to interrupt." Hank said, his white

beard glowing silver in the candle-light. "I just wanted to tell you that she's here. Right outside the chapel."

"Great!" Jessa gave Hank a big hug. "Thanks again, Hank. My dad should be arriving any minute."

"I'll meet you outside, then." Hank said, adjusting his cowboy hat and weaving back through the crowd.

"Who's here?" Jay asked, puzzled.

"Come on, I'll show you." Jessa took his hand and pulled him to the door. As she stepped out into the night, she saw that the stars had started to come out, tiny pin-pricks in a black sky. All around them the spruce-tops towered in craggy points. Just left of the chapel, Barb stood in her usual slicker and cowboy hat, holding Fairlight on a lead-rope. As Jessa and Jay walked towards her, she heard her dad's truck rumbling towards them on the wide mulched trail.

"Hey, girlie." Jessa cooed and patted Fairlight on the nose. "How are you doing? Do you remember Jay?" Fairlight nuzzled Jessa's hand as Barb passed her the lead rope. Jay patted Fairlight's neck, still looking confused.

"What's she doing way up here at this hour?" Jay said. "Shouldn't she be out to pasture?"

"I bought her this afternoon." Jessa beamed. "Hank and I just finished the paper-work a couple of hours ago. She's mine. That's my dad coming with a trailer to pick her up." She gestured at the headlights as they came closer.

"Wow, that's awesome!" Jay said. "Congratulations!"

"Someone pulled a few strings for me." Jessa winked at Barb. "And my dad is helping me out, too." Barb spoke, then, as mysterious and poetically as ever.

For who can separate
The truest of loves
For all blessed friendships
Are from the Father, above
No man can destroy
The bond you two share

For you belong to each other
By the depth of your care.

"Thanks, Barb." Jessa said softly. "And thanks for convincing Hank to let me buy her. I know you must have had a hand in that."

"You know I can't turn down my angel for anything." Hank said, walking over to her. "Here, Jessa, I'll help your dad get her loaded in trailer." He took Fairlight's rope from Barb.

"Thanks for everything, Hank." Jessa said. "I mean it."

"I'm proud of you, Jessa." Hank said. "Take good care of Fairlight."

"I will." Jessa promised.

"And you take good care of Jessa, young man." He said to Jay, then turned with Barb to lead Fairlight into the trailer.

Jay grasped Jessa's hand tighter and pulled it to his lips to kiss it softly. Jessa thought she could hear her heart singing. With his eyes full of promise, Jay leaned closer to whisper in her ear, "I will."

The End

DON'T MISS BOOKS ONE AND TWO IN THE SUMMER TRAILS SERIES

Book 1: Summer Trails

Sixteen-year-old Jessa Davies is going to horse camp; and this year she's on staff! She can't wait to spend her summer as a wrangler; riding her favorite horse, goofing off with friends, and basically having a blast. Things go even better than expected when the cutest cowboy at camp starts paying special attention to her!

But things get complicated fast when a co-worker seems to hate her guts. Jessa starts to question everything; from her crush, to whether she even has what it takes to be a wrangler. Tempers run high as manipulation clouds the truth, and Jessa wonders why she ever thought wrangling was good idea. Through it all she is reminded of God´s love as she rides along the summer trails.

Book 2: Trails in the Wilderness

Jessa Davies is back, and she's going horse-camping! She's been given a special assignment at the remote teepee camp, where she and Marsha will be leaders. Jessa worries about the responsibility of being a counselor when a new problem arises; a gorgeous newcomer threatens to steal Wade's attention. What's more, a sullen camper and a dark mystery threaten to destroy everything Jessa cares about.

As things go from bad to worse, Jessa has to make a decision: to hold on tight to what she wants, or to trust God and let go.

ABOUT THE AUTHOR

Janessa Suderman grew up going to horse camp in the foothills of southern Alberta, Canada, and remembers those years fondly. She bought her first horse Dawn at the age of 16, and still gets out riding on her as often as possible. Janessa received her Bachelor of Science in Nursing Degree from Trinity Western University, and works part-time as a nurse. An avid reader from a young age, Janessa kept her younger brother entertained by making up elaborate stories to help him get to sleep. Over the years she has written multiple short stories, poetry, and novels for leisure. The Summer Trails Series is her first published work. She currently lives in southern Alberta with her husband and young son.

Made in the USA
Middletown, DE
24 April 2017